10, 9, 8, 7, 6, 5, 4, 3, 2, 1 . . . we have lift-off !

Blast off into space and meet . . . Talia, who is determined to escape from a planet where she is forced to live as an outsider; Tony, whose brother's body is taken over by an alien; Trel and Zawn, hostages in space; and many other amazing characters.

This brilliant collection of original stories comes from a rocketful of top authors, including Nicholas Fisk, Malorie Blackman, Douglas Hill, Mary Hoffman and Helen Dunmore. It's out of this world!

Also available by Tony Bradman,
and published by Corgi Books:

A STACK OF STORY POEMS

GOOD SPORTS! A BAG OF SPORTS STORIES

AMAZING ADVENTURE STORIES

FANTASTIC SPACE STORIES

COLLECTED BY
TONY BRADMAN

Illustrated by Jon Riley

CORGI

CORGI BOOKS

FANTASTIC SPACE STORIES
A CORGI BOOK : 0 552 52767 X

First published in Great Britain by Doubleday,
a division of Transworld Publishers Ltd

PRINTING HISTORY
Doubleday edition published 1994
Corgi edition published 1995
Corgi edition reprinted 1996

Corgi Books are published by Transworld Publishers Ltd,
61–63 Uxbridge Road, Ealing, London W5 5SA,
in Australia by Transworld Publishers (Australia) Pty Ltd,
15–25 Helles Avenue, Moorebank, NSW 2170
and in New Zealand by Transworld Publishers (NZ) Ltd,
3 William Pickering Drive, Albany, Auckland.

Printed and bound in Great Britain by
Cox & Wyman Ltd, Reading, Berkshire.

CONTENTS

FLIGHT FOR FREEDOM
by Sue Welford

Inside the hangar it was as dark as a razor-rat's hole. At one end, a crack in the panels let in a single, bright shaft of light. It looked like an escape route from hell.

Even though she stood on tiptoe, Talia's eye was only just level with the broken window. She balanced precariously on a pile of garbage – rusting cans, old clothes, bones, the skull of a giant silvertail. She had already fallen once, cutting her knee badly. She had sworn loudly then fumbled about in one of her pockets for medi-plast. All she'd got was her mastercode-key, her knife, several flashlighters. Pretty standard equipment for a street kid. In one pocket she found the other half of the mouldy bread roll she'd had for breakfast. She'd been saving it for lunch.

1

The roll would probably be all Talia would have to eat that day.

Talia craned her neck. She HAD to get inside the hangar, had to find out what was in there if it was the last thing in this world she ever did. She'd always had the strange feeling something waited for her out in these dark and deserted desolate regions, something that might change her life for ever.

The night was cold. At this time of year, the temperature regulators didn't work this far out. The inner precincts of the city were warm enough, but here in the outer limits, it was like the legendary winters of the old home-planet Talia's mother had told her about. Nothing survived out here for long. Only razors, silvertails, the odd family of garbage-dragons. The cold was bitter, damp. Talia's hair stuck to her forehead. She fell again as the heap of filth collapsed beneath her. She cursed, kicking out angrily. The skull of the giant silvertail rolled into the gutter.

Talia had never been out this far before. A Wanderer, a street-child, Talia had been into almost every forbidden precinct before she was ten years old. Some said ghosts lurked in these outer regions. Spirits of people, long-dead. People stranded in time warps created by shock waves and radiation. Talia wasn't frightened of legends. Her parents had been terminated when she was three years old. There had been a slave uprising, a mass attempt to escape. Her

2

parents were caught trying to board a starfreighter bound for their home-planet. Ever since then, Talia had known it was the living you should be scared of. Not the dead.

Glancing over her shoulder in case any foot-patrols hunted the area, Talia crept round to the side of the building. There *was* something in there, she knew it. She *had* to get inside.

A startled garbage-dragon hissed at her, annoyed by the sudden appearance of a stranger in its territory. It lashed its tail then flew away on wings of midnight. Talia watched. Seeing a creature soar into the air like that made her think about her parents. About their people, their life before capture into mutilation and slavery . . . The dragon's fiery breath lit up the dark sky like a flare. Talia saw it settle, crowing on the outstretched, petrified branch of a long-dead poplash tree. It began to preen its scales, its spiked silhouette dark against the stars. Talia shrugged and turned away.

Suddenly a shaft of light appeared above. The garbage-dragon gave a squawk and flew off. It disappeared over the ruined horizon. Talia crouched, making herself small against the wall of the hangar. She put her arms over her face and head. If the patrol spotted her they'd shoot on sight. Patrol-droids never asked questions. Talia shivered. She pulled her jackets tighter round her thin, humped body.

The vehicle hovered ten metres above the

3

ground. The down-draught from its thrusters caused a hurricane of dust and dirt. Talia saw the patrol-droid jump out, huge searchbeam sweeping across to the place where she crouched. Its dark figure was silhouetted against the brightness like the angel of death. Talia froze. Waiting. Breath held for the sound of laser-fire. None came. Peeping through a veil of tangled hair, Talia saw the droid signal the pilot. The sky-car hovered just long enough for it to jump back inside then it whirled away. The air throbbed then settled into silence.

When she was sure the sky-car had gone, Talia stood. She heaved a sigh of relief. She clambered on to a twist of metal that might have once been a chair and stretched upward. She dug her fingers into the side of a loose panel. She wrenched. The panel came away, edges crumbling, rusting in her fingers. Talia scrambled up, through and into the dark, silent building. Now, at last, she would find out what was inside.

Talia hadn't known there were any of these old hangars left. She had always imagined everything this far out had been totally destroyed in the zone wars. A scuttling in the corner told Talia the place was infested. Silvertails. Probably razor-rats as well. There might even be a scag waiting to spring, jaws snapping, from one of the dim corners. Talia fingered her knife warily. Way above, skylight windows dotted the sloping roof. Through the broken glass Talia could see the stars, the three moons of the planet glowing golden. She lifted her arms as if to reach for them. Then she took a flashlighter from her pocket and pulled the tab. The sharp, blue glow showed something looming ahead. Talia picked her way carefully across the rubbish-strewn floor. She drew in her breath. Towering above her was the hull of a giant vessel of some kind. Eyes adjusting to the semi-darkness she could just make it out. The gleaming silver-metal reflected the stars. The sharp, elegant point of its nose was thrust towards her. The wings, swept back like those of a great bird, were painted scarlet . . . Talia knew immediately what it was. A starship. She had heard stories of starships. How they had ferried to and fro across the galaxies in the days when this world was at peace. Before its inhabitants had set out to conquer the universe. Talia had seen a picture of a ship like this once. It was in a newsmag gleaned from the bottom of a rubbish bin. She remembered it had filled her with a sense of longing. A desperate need to be flying free, to escape for ever the gutters of her existence. Talia frowned, trying to remember the starship's name . . . She lit another flashlighter. The glare illuminated the lettering on the side. *Starskimmer I*. That was it! There had been a story too, but it had been written in a language Talia couldn't read. The flashlighter showed something else. A ladder, leading to the cockpit. Talia's heart drummed with excitement. If she could just get inside . . .

It was a long climb. Up there, Talia looked down. A dragon's eye view of the world. The sound of the returning sky-car catapulted Talia into action. Using her mastercode-key to activate the hatch she climbed inside the cockpit and ducked down out of sight.

Zenas opened the hangar doors. Afternoon light streamed in. He stood on the threshold looking at *Starskimmer I*. There was no doubt about it; the old bus looked great. Zenas sighed. His job here was just about finished. Mind you, he'd be glad to get back to the city. These outer zones really gave him the creeps.

Half-way up the cockpit ladder, Zenas took a rag from the back pocket of his flightsuit and leaned over to rub an imaginary speck of dust from *Starskimmer*'s shining hull. He felt a thrill of excitement, of pride. The kind of feeling he used to have when he regularly ferried this old bus to and fro across the third galaxy. A real cool pilot he'd been, the best in the Fleet. He still held the record for the fastest run between Io and Ganmedia although no-one remembered it now-adays. No-one had been more sorry than he had when the route became too dangerous to run and the *Starskimmer* fleet was grounded for what he'd thought was for ever.

Zenas tipped his cap on to the back of his head. He snorted. Now they were re-running one of the old star-routes for some kind of victory celebrations. Victory! What kind of victory was it when half the damned planet was in ruins and the other half was peopled by power-mad maniacs and slaves, most of those poor creatures mutilated beyond recognition to prevent their escape.

Zenas sighed and continued his slow climb to the cockpit. There was a time when he'd shin up like a swing-monkey. He grinned to himself. An old-timer like him re-fitting the old girl, AND flying her memorial trip. They'd brought him out of retirement to do it. The whole idea seemed crazy to him, spending all those credits on one meagre space flight. But Zenas had learned a long time ago . . . it was very unwise to argue.

The cockpit hatch was open. Zenas frowned. He felt sure he'd locked it the night before. He shrugged. Maybe he'd forgotten. His memory sure wasn't what it used to be. No-one came to the outer precincts anyway. A few Wanderers maybe. A few Fugitives. None of them lasted long once patrols spotted them. Zenas took out his code-key and opened the inner hatch to the pilot's cabin. The seat still fitted around his lean body as if it had been made for him. He looked at the vast array of buttons and display units. He was going to try her today. Just taxi her out to the launch pad. Then, tomorrow, the short trip to the inner precinct spaceport so some VIP could give a speech before they took off. Zenas felt a thrill of anticipation. Felt the adrenalin shoot through his veins. He felt young again, sitting in his captain's seat. A real hot-shot flyer cruising those stars . . . He reached to the overhead panel and punched in a code. There was a hiss of static, a flash of white. Somewhere in the aft cabin a klaxon screamed a warning. Loud enough to wake the dead. Zenas swore under his breath. He'd got to get everything functioning before tomorrow or else he'd go the way of everyone else who didn't do their job properly. Zenas made a face and drew his forefinger across his throat grimly. Then he punched another code and the screen went blank. Suddenly, to his surprise, a hiss, a soft clunk, told him a hatch had opened behind him. He turned, frowning. His hand reached for the shooter in his belt. If a damn silvertail'd got in here he'd blast it to hell.

A figure stepped through. It looked like a kid. An off-worlder, Zenas felt sure. No native of this planet looked like her. She was dressed in black. Torn leggings, bulky, steel-studded leather jackets. As she came forward Zenas saw it wasn't really a kid at all. Just a small person, a teen maybe. Definitely an off-worlder though. He could tell by her huge eyes and that crest of black hair. She was slightly bent over as if she carried a burden on her back. He wondered how she got here; he hadn't known there were any of her race left on this planet. He thought they'd all been killed in the uprisings of a decade ago. Those that hadn't died already whilst being operated on. She was staring at him, eyes wide with shock. She crouched, then turned to run.

Zenas flipped a button on the arm of his seat and the hatch hissed shut.

'Hey!' The girl turned back quickly. She reminded him of a bird, the way her head was tilted to one side, huge eyes darting to and fro. A knife appeared in her hand as if she had materialized it from thin air.

'Let me out!' she hissed.

'Not until you tell me what the hell you're doing here.'

'I fell asleep. I haven't pinched anything.' She stepped towards him. 'Let me out or else I'll . . .' She held the knife up. In spite of the harshness of her fear, her voice had a musical quality. Zenas had heard something like it somewhere before but, just for the minute, he couldn't remember where.

Zenas shook his head. 'How the hell did you get in?'

The girl hesitated. Zenas saw her relax a little. Then she shrugged. 'I climbed up. Think I flew, did you?'

Zenas sighed. They were all the same. Youngsters. All disrespectful. Alien or otherwise. He supposed she was a Wanderer, and Wanderers got in anywhere.

The girl's huge eyes scoured the cabin. Then she looked back at him.

'You the pilot?' she asked.

In spite of his annoyance Zenas felt a thrill of pride. 'Sure am,' he said.

'I didn't know they used these starships any more, not since linear-drive was invented.'

'They don't,' he said gruffly, 'I've restored her for a special voyage tomorrow.'

'Oh.' The girl relaxed. She came over and slid into the seat beside him. She fiddled with the impact harness, trying to fix it together.

'Here . . .' Zenas leaned across and buckled it for her. She wriggled deeply into the seat. She didn't fit into it like he did. Her back was a different shape. She was the only one of her kind Zenas had ever seen that hadn't been disfigured. Her feet swung above the floor, heavy boots kicking.

She looked at him and grinned. 'Feels great. How does she . . . ?' Talia leaned forward and touched the panel.

'Hey, don't touch anything!'

'Why not?'

Zenas shrugged. He didn't know why not. You just told kids not to touch things in case they broke them. His grandkids seemed to break everything they were given. 'Just keep your mitts off,' he growled.

The girl swivelled her seat round. Then back again as if she was on a fairground ride. 'Why are you in a bad temper?'

11

Zenas frowned. What kind of damn fool question was that? 'I'm not,' he said.

'Well, you don't seem very happy. You should be, you know. Getting to go on a space voyage. Want to swap places?' Talia grinned.

Zenas frowned again. He wasn't used to youngsters. Especially ones who accused him of being crotchety. His grandkids lived on Mallia V. He only saw them now and again. When he did see them they got on his nerves.

'Are you kidding?' he said.

The girl stretched out a hand. She touched his arm. Her fingers were slender, almost clawlike. Dirty. She smiled at him. 'Show me how to fly her?' she warbled. 'Please . . . ?'

'Taking her up's easy,' he said modestly. He pointed to the screen. 'The codes come up. It's once you get into deep space, it's then you hit trouble if you don't know the ropes.'

'Just show me the codes,' Talia begged.

Zenas shrugged. What harm could it do?

Zenas punched in a code. A thin whine cut through the cockpit as *Starskimmer*'s engines awoke from their long sleep. Talia clutched the arms of her seat. Another set of codes flashed. Zenas punched buttons without glancing at the screen.

'Are you taking her out now?'

Zenas shook his head. 'Later. There's a couple of

12

adjustments . . .' He punched another code and the engines died.

'That's great!' Talia's eyes shone.

Suddenly Zenas found himself telling her things. How he'd been the captain who'd clocked up the most space miles during his service to the Fleet. It had been a long time since anyone had been interested in his stories. He was just about to tell her about his skirmish with the robo-warriors from Zeta V, his run-in with the Centaurian Watchdog when she interrupted him.

'Tomorrow . . . ? Where you going?'

'To the city spaceport.'

'Which one?'

Zenas told her. He explained about the ceremony. Then about the trip to Ganmedia.

'You couldn't . . . ?'

He looked at the girl. Her dark-brown eyes were round and shining. 'What?'

'Show me some more . . . take me up . . . a kind of trial run if you like.'

'Without permission? Are you kidding?' Zenas laughed. 'You know what happens to folk who do things without permission.'

'They wouldn't know, would they?'

'Of course they'd know,' he answered bitterly. 'They know everything on this damned planet, don't they?'

'If you hate it so much,' the girl said softly, 'why don't you escape?'

He looked at Talia. 'Why don't you?'

'I don't have a starship. You do.'

Zenas didn't answer. The girl was right. The question had hovered like a wing-beetle at the back of Zenas' mind ever since being assigned to the job. He didn't even have anywhere particular in mind. Just to be out there, flying free amongst the stars. Just cruising deep space. Away from this stinking planet he used to be proud to come home to. He shook his head. 'You're crazy.' he said.

'Did you ever go to the planet Avisia?' she asked suddenly.

Zenas nodded. 'Once.' He looked at Talia knowingly. 'That's where you came from, isn't it?'

Talia shook her head. 'Not me . . . my parents. I was born here.' She told Zenas how she had been left for dead when her parents were killed.

'So you've never seen your home-planet?'

'My mother told me stories . . . about open spaces and freedom and . . . peace.' Talia hung her head.

Zenas touched her shoulder in sympathy. 'They were all true, kid. All those stories were true.'

But the girl wasn't listening. She had her head cocked to one side. She began to tear frantically at her harness. 'Get me out,' she hissed. 'I can hear them coming.'

Zenas unlocked the belts. Talia jumped from the

seat and fled to the hatch, her jackets flapping like wings around her. She hesitated, turned. 'Zenas . . . ?'

'Yeah?' Zenas almost knew what she was going to say.

'Can't you . . . ? Can't we . . . ?'

Zenas shook his head. His voice was full of regret. 'I don't think so, kid.'

'But you'd be free, Zenas.'

Zenas shook his head. 'I'm too old . . .'

Talia ran back. She crouched by his pilots' chair, gazing upwards at him.

'Zenas, you're not too old. You're never too old to be free.' When he didn't answer, Talia stood up. She shrugged. 'OK. I understand. I know what it is to be scared.'

Scared? Who me, the hot-shot flyer? Zenas opened his mouth to reply but she had gone.

Outside, it was twilight. The usual gloom of evening settled over the outer precincts like the threat of a storm. The air throbbed with the sound of the sky-car. Talia dodged along the side of the hangar, crouching low, hump-backed, towards the doorway. A hundred metres away a dark-suited patrol-droid swung down. Its infra-red would have to be malfunctioning not to pick her up.

Watching from above, a vision flashed into Zenas' mind. The planet Avisia. Green fields, trees, rainbow-flowers, blue water . . . He saw its people, remembered their welcome . . . their music . . .

Talia crouched in the doorway. She swore under her breath. She must have been crazy. Why didn't she MAKE that old man take her out. She could have hijacked that ship, no trouble. She fingered her knife. It was almost night. Outside, the sky-car settled into hover mode and a second patroller jumped from the cab and made towards the hangar. It stood on the threshold, looking round. Talia saw it set its laser on kill.

Talia pressed herself against the wall. There was no way out. If she dodged past the droid it would spot her for sure. If she tried to get out the way she'd got in, the one scouting outside would get her. Blast her before she'd gone twenty metres. She looked up. There was only one way out . . . and that was . . . *up*.

A ricochet of hot air blew across Talia's crouching body. The ship was beginning to move, taxi-ing slowly across the hangar towards the open doors. Zenas was taking *Starskimmer* out. Tomorrow the ship would be spacebound for the first time in twenty years. What was it Zenas had said? Flying free . . .

And then, suddenly, Talia knew what she must do. She'd only done it once before. That time she'd been careless enough to let a patroller discover her pinching stuff from a food warehouse in the thirteenth precinct. It had been easy . . . so easy . . . but she had never dared do it again for fear of being spotted. More than death, Talia was scared of the surgical operation that had made so many of her kind so helpless.

Talia drew a deep breath. She glanced towards the open doors. The patrol-droid had gone the other way but it was only a matter of time before it spotted her.

Wrenching off her belt she threw it aside. Suddenly, the patroller appeared in the shadowed doorway. Its shouted command was lost beneath the high pitched whine of *Starskimmer*'s engines.

Talia shrugged off her jackets and kicked off her heavy boots. Behind her, the burden she'd kept hidden all her life unfolded and stretched. Talia stood on tiptoe. She twisted her body, testing stiff muscles. Then she bent her knees and leapt forwards. Her wings flapped once. Then again as she soared upwards towards *Starskimmer*'s cockpit. The hatch was still open. A burst of laser-fire skittered harmlessly past *Starskimmer*'s wing as Talia clambered inside.

Zenas didn't turn. The inner hatch hissed shut. Talia's wings folded together and settled against her back. She stood silently watching his fingers deftly punching codes. She wondered if he even knew she was there. She approached him cautiously. He didn't even flinch as she held her knife to his throat.

'You've got to get me out of here, Zenas,' she hissed.

Zenas grinned to himself. As if some desperate kid

could hijack a starship. She was crazier than he'd thought.

'Put the knife away, Talia,' he said calmly. 'I've decided to take your advice.'

'Huh?' Talia didn't move.

Ignoring the blade, cold against the skin of his throat, Zenas stretched towards the overhead panel and flicked a switch.

He heard the hesitation in Talia's voice. 'What are you going to do?'

'What do you think I'm going to do?'

Zenas felt the knife drop away. 'I don't know.' In Talia's voice Zenas heard all the hopelessness of her life.

He smiled and patted the seat beside him. 'I'm going to take you home.'

Out on the launch pad, Zenas hit the thrusters. *Starskimmer* responded with a deafening roar. Together, Zenas and Talia watched the hangar . . . the patrollers . . . the sky-car . . . the ruined horizon . . . dwindle into nothingness until all they could see was the wide midnight-blue of the sky and the beckoning stars.

BARRY
by Stephen Bowkett

When my parents told me that we were hosting a family from Earth, I didn't know whether to be glad, or to sulk or just lose my temper.

I mean, there's not much to do on Mars at the best of times. It was going to be hard work looking after some kid who was used to green grass and fresh air and millions of people. And anyway, I valued my spare time. I liked reading and computers. And I enjoyed going out to Viewpoint Rock to do some stargazing (that's if we weren't in the middle of a sandstorm! Mars is pretty famous for those, as you probably know).

On the other hand, I didn't have many friends here in the colony. Life could be pretty lonely . . . But what if I just didn't get on with him, or he with me? It was a real gamble.

So I decided to lose my temper.

'It's not fair,' I said, folding my arms tight to show how cross I was. 'I spend hours doing my school-work. I keep my room tidy, and I do my share of the housework – I don't have the time to babymind an Earthsider!'

Dad listened to all of this patiently enough, while Mum sat there and tried not to take sides. I suppose they could have pulled rank on me and simply made it an order. But instead, Dad's voice went very quiet and serious. He was treating me as an adult, even though I was behaving like a child.

'Kevin, you've been learning in school about the Star-Rider Project, haven't you?'

I nodded, letting my temper cool. 'It's man's first flight to the stars. No-one has ever left the solar system before. Star-Rider isn't just one spaceship, it's a cluster of them. They were built in Moon orbit and have been flown to Mars for final launch in—' I checked my wristo. 'In three months.'

'OK, fine. Well, you probably also know that almost all of those ships are automatic: they're the labs and the fuel tankers and so on. Only one ship will have people aboard – the family who will be staying with us. Then they'll be leaving the sun and its planets behind for ever . . .'

'You mean—'

20

Dad nodded. 'That's right, Kevin. The Bradburys are making a one-way journey. They will never return, because the stars are so very far away . . .'

'And you'll find them very pleasant,' Mum added, as my temper faded completely and wonder took its place. 'Look, I have a picture . . .'

And she showed me. Two nice normal-looking parents and a boy of about my age. Thinking about it, I reckoned we'd get on together just fine.

We went to the dock to greet them. We watched from the observation lounge as the big shuttle-freighter thundered down from orbit. It was a huge craft, robot-controlled. It kicked up plenty of Mars' red sand as it settled on the pad. A little beetle-shaped transporter drove across to ferry-off the passengers. Stores would be unloaded later.

I felt nervous waiting with Mum and Dad at Reception. The Bradburys would need to undergo the usual checks, but it shouldn't take long in their case, Dad said.

Soon, the inner airlock door slid open and they came through – looking as nervous as we did. Dad went over and shook hands with Mr Bradbury, then Mrs Bradbury. He smiled at their son. Then Mum did the same. All very polite and friendly.

Then it was my turn. Dad beckoned me forward.

'And can I introduce you to our son, Kevin. Kev to his friends.'

'So I hope you'll call me Kev,' I said, thinking that sounded very clever.

'Hello, Kev,' Mr Bradbury said, beaming a big smile at me. 'We're really pleased to meet you. And thank you, thank you all, for agreeing to put us up. Kev,' Mr Bradbury added, 'this is Barry.'

The boy stepped forward. He was taller than me and stronger-looking. His hair was very blond, his eyes very blue.

For a second or two, I didn't know how he was going to react. The next three months could either be great fun, or just plain dreadful . . .

Barry held out his hand and we shook, sort of seriously. But I knew then, somehow, that things were going to be all right. I knew that Barry needed a friend as much as I did. After all, outer space is the loneliest place there is.

'Well, that's grand.' Dad rubbed his hands together briskly. 'Let's go back home and relax. We can do the tour later. Kevin's just dying to show you Clarkesville, Barry. Right, Kev?'

'Right, Dad,' I agreed, but not really. I'd much rather be playing with my computer.

'So there's not that much to Clarkesville – but it's home . . .' I could've bitten my tongue, then, at what I'd said. 'I'm sorry, Barry. I shouldn't have said that. I guess you're feeling pretty homesick already, aren't you?'

Barry shrugged. 'I'm not sick of home,' he said. 'I don't actually *have* a home. I suppose that Star-Rider will be my home . . .'

'That's not quite how I meant it . . . But never mind. I'll show you the West Window. It looks out over Viewpoint Rock, which is where I like to go sometimes. Then we can finish the tour tomorrow. You've got three months with us, after all. Maybe later,' I added hopefully, 'we could play on my computer.'

'Yes,' Barry agreed, 'if you like. But I don't play on computers much. I work with them.'

'I promise you'll enjoy the games,' I told him. 'Let's see if you can beat my high score on *Galaxy Raiders*.'

Barry smiled. I couldn't tell if he was making fun of me or not . . .

The West Window gives you the best view of Mars you can get from Clarkesville. It's also the place where a lot of the kids at the base tend to meet. There are some autovendors and a music system, so it's used as a bit of a social centre.

The place was quite busy when we got there. I knew most of the kids who were hanging around. Some of them were OK, but there were a few I would rather have avoided, Don Golding among them.

Don Golding is my sworn enemy, although I didn't really know why. It all seemed to start about a year ago, when I beat his high score on the *Alien*

Attack game . . . I suppose it didn't help when I topped his best on *Robot Revenge* a couple of days later . . .

But since then, Don has tried to beat me in other ways.

'Who's this, then?' Don asked in a sneery sort of way. Some of the people around him sniggered. 'Has your dad paid for someone to be your friend?'

'This is Barry Bradbury,' I replied calmly. 'And no-one's paid anybody for anything.' I was trying to be as friendly as possible, but Don and his cronies weren't making it easy. There was trouble coming. I just knew it.

I turned to Barry. 'I'll get drinks for us,' I muttered, determined not to run away from Don Golding and his bullying. I had run away from him too many times before.

When I reached the drinks' machine, I realized I hadn't asked Barry what he liked. I got two colas anyway, turned to walk back – and my heart sank.

Don and his group of followers had walked over to Barry, and Don was talking quickly and was jabbing his finger near his face. Barry was just standing there and smiling, as though he hadn't a clue what was going on.

'. . . so I'm just telling you—' I caught that scrap of Don's angry sentence and my temper flared.

'Don,' I snapped, ignoring my own nervousness,

'that's enough! Barry's a visitor to Mars. Be polite, even if you can't be friendly. Just leave him alone, and stop behaving like a child!'

Don grinned nastily. 'Are you going to make me stop? Well, yellow belly – do you think you can?'

'Look, I don't want trouble . . .' I began quietly. It sounded pathetic. I could feel myself shaking, and Don had that mean and menacing look about him. It was fight or run.

'I don't care what you want, little cowardy-Kevin. But this is what you're going to get—'

Don's fist drew back. I waited for it to squash my nose, but the blow never arrived. Barry's arm had shot out and stopped it in midair.

'Leave him alone. He hasn't hurt you.'

Barry was amazingly calm, and had moved with even more amazing speed. Don's mouth dropped open for an instant – then he snarled and turned his temper on Barry. He lashed out with a crippling kick—

But Barry wasn't there. He'd somehow stepped aside in a flicker of motion, so that Don stumbled and fell flat-out in a sprawl.

Some of the kids nearby started to laugh. Then they shut up again as Don scrambled to his feet and jumped at Barry with a high kick (which any fool can do on low-gravity Mars).

Barry performed the miracle again. As Don sailed towards him, Barry grabbed his leg, swung him around in a great arc and sent him spinning away. He landed right by the drinks' machines in a knot of arms and legs. Don's nose started to bleed.

'Come on Barry,' I said, knowing our luck wouldn't last. 'Let's get out of here. These goons have shown how stupid they can be, and that's about all!'

I grabbed his arm and led him away, not even bothering to cast a triumphant glance over my shoulder. It would not have been the wise thing to do. Barry had made some friends in beating the loutish Don Golding. But he'd made some enemies, too. And serious ones at that.

Dinner that night was strange. I suppose it was partly my fault. I just didn't want to talk about the trouble with Don, although Barry couldn't understand that. It was OK for him, he could handle himself. And besides, when the Bradbury family had departed on their journey to the stars, I'd still be here. Me and Don Golding and his bullying.

But there was something else that spoiled things a little. I didn't know quite what it was for a time, but then I understood. As Mr Bradbury talked more about the Star-Rider Project, I saw that my father was jealous.

Afterwards, as we all sat in the lounge while the house-droid washed the dishes, Dad and Mr Bradbury got talking. Mum and Mrs Bradbury started up a conversation by themselves. Barry and I found ourselves listening to our fathers.

'I don't know,' Dad said, shaking his head. 'I just don't know how you folks can stand leaving everything behind . . . your home, your friends, your roots, everything that's familiar and safe . . . I mean, good heavens, what if there's an emergency on the ship? Why, you couldn't even—'

'Dad!' I broke in, stopping the foolish words before they were spoken. 'The Star-Rider Project has taken over ten years to plan. Nothing will go wrong . . . OK?'

He realized what he'd been about to say, and put his coffee mug gently down.

'Um, yes, that's right. Of course . . . I meant to say that I admire your bravery. It takes a lot of courage to do what you're doing. I was looking on the black side. Stupid of me . . . To tell you the truth, I wish *I* was going on that journey.'

'We see it as a duty,' Mr Bradbury pointed out quietly. 'Courage doesn't come into it at all.'

'Excitement, then – the sheer thrill of going to the stars! Heck,' Dad grinned, 'my life is astronomy. That's why I came out to Mars. I feel a bit closer to the sky here, if you know what I mean. But to go there! What must it feel like . . . ?'

'More coffee anyone?' I said it loudly and stood up as I spoke. Mr Bradbury started to shake his head, then changed his mind and nodded.

'Yes, I will. Thank you.'

'I'll help you, Kev,' Barry offered. I suppose he was embarrassed as well, to see my father rambling on so much . . . Although I was also curious about the answer to Dad's question!

We went through to the kitchen.

The house-droid had finished the dinner things and had stacked itself neatly in a corner niche. I clattered about with the cutlery, feeling awkward with Barry standing there behind me.

'Is everything all right, Kev?' Barry asked. Maybe he didn't understand how my father felt, in the same way that Dad couldn't figure the Bradburys.

'I suppose it is really . . . I just feel I want to apologize for the way Dad's been. I think he can't work out why you aren't scared or excited, or anything. *He* sure is, and he isn't making the trip! He can only look at the stars through his telescope. He's worried for your safety, and Mum is, and I am . . . You are brave, all of you, whether you admit it or not . . . And I know you must be scared really, deep down . . . You are only human, after all . . .'

Then Barry smiled. And something awful happened in my heart. I knew that the idea that came to me then was true. Utterly and completely true. It shocked me rigid, so that I dropped the coffee cup I was holding.

The house-droid whirred and sped forward, chromium tendrils uncoiling . . .

But Barry got to it first.

Fear stopped me from asking him straight out. But that night, deep in the early hours when the house was silent, I crept into his room and walked over to look at him.

Barry had left his bedside computer screen switched on. Numbers and letters were whizzing past more quickly than my eye could follow them. I glanced at the screen, then at Barry. A cable ran between them, entering a socket at Barry's temple, normally hidden by his hairline. His eyes were closed, as though in sleep, but he was not breathing. I knew he couldn't be.

I felt cold suddenly, and began to shake. I turned to leave, determined never to speak to him again after the way he'd tricked me . . . But the screen bleeped as I was half-way to the door. I turned and read the message which had appeared there:

DON'T TELL YOUR PARENTS, KEV. THEY WOULD NEVER UNDERSTAND. I AM STILL YOUR FRIEND. TRULY.

I closed Barry's door, returned to my bed, and stayed awake until morning.

'You fooled us all,' I said. I couldn't bear to look at him. 'You and your parents, except they aren't your parents at all; they can't be! And the people who built you fooled us, too. Was it someone's idea of a joke, to make androids so perfect that we couldn't tell you're machines?'

It sounded spiteful and mean coming out the way it did, but that's how I felt. Somehow – cheated.

'But we're not perfect, Kev. That's why we came to Mars to stay with a human family. To learn from you. The Star-Rider Project is possible only with androids, because we don't sleep, and we need no food. We don't die. But we need to feel what people feel – to experience the awe and wonder of the galaxy. How else can we tell you properly what we find out there?'

It all sounded very logical, but I wasn't sure I was convinced. We said nothing more for a while, as we walked through the outer zone of Clarkesville and came at last to The Garden.

Like most of the areas of the colony, The Garden was sealed off by airlocks. We went through these and into a large domed chamber, rather like a great glasshouse. It was filled with shadows and green growing plants and the sweet smell of soil.

'It's where the agrilab technicians do a lot of their experiments,' I explained. 'But the public is allowed in – it's one of the few places on Mars that makes you feel like you're on Earth!

'Is that why you brought me here, then, to taunt me?'

I glared at him, at his flawless face and his shining eyes that seemed so human, even though I knew they weren't.

'You have a lot to learn about us, Barry,' I said. 'Maybe I came here to taunt myself . . .'

'I don't understand that,' he replied. And a fresh wave of hurt burst inside me.

'You mean "It does not compute"?'

Now it was his turn to smile.

'You have a lot to learn about us,' Barry said. And I smiled also, because no simple machine would ever have said that.

Barry was about to say something else. But then he stared past me and was gone from sight, before I could blink.

'Barry – what—'

'No. NO!' he yelled. I caught sight of him like a flash of colour in the green gloom. A red light came on above the airlock door as he reached it – and smashed his fist hard into it, denting the metal.

Then it registered in my head. A red emergency light.

At first you could hardly feel the loss of air pressure: just a tickling in the lungs, a faint popping of the ears. The fronds and tall leaves around me stirred in a breeze that would grow to a storm – and then to silence as the atmosphere in the chamber gushed out. Finally, it would be impossible to breathe. Impossible to live. I wondered if it would be a painful way to die, and a bright white panic caught light in my chest and began burning through my body . . .

Then I saw who was looking at us from the observation window, and the panic faded. Barry was still hammering on the door, metal to metal. If he damaged it much more it wouldn't open when the time came – as I knew it would. Don Golding was out to have his silly revenge, to scare us, that was all. It was just a waiting game.

I hurried over to Barry and pulled him away, explaining the trick Don had played on us.

'In a few moments he'll reckon we've suffered enough, and let us out.'

'I see,' Barry said, and disappeared into the shrubbery.

I was right. The door slid open. Then the inner door. I stepped out to see Don's smug, triumphant grin – which died on his face as he realized I was alone.

'K-Kevin . . .' stammered Don, his face turning as pale as paper. 'W-where's B-Barry?'

Then he turned and tried to run from the scene of his crime.

'You're a fool, Don,' I spat at him. 'You always were, and you always will be.'

I leaped at him, grabbed his collar and shoved him back up to the window. And we both watched Barry standing there among the foliage, laughing when he should have been dying.

I guess Don learned his lesson, then.

I guess we all did.

Now I stand on Viewpoint Rock with Mum and Dad, sealed in a spacesuit, my visor pulled down so that no-one can see my tears. At any moment the great Star-Rider engines will explode into furious life, and start the ships on their path to the heavens.

I think back to my last hour with Barry. We played computer games, which he won easily. I told him not to let me beat him, just because I was a human. Nor did he. He just grinned and said teasingly, 'You don't stand a chance, Kev. This machine's like a brother to me . . .'

I like to think I helped him find his sense of humour. He'll need it, where he's going.

And – there! The engines have fired and a comet-trail of brilliance spreads across the sky. The ship-cluster begins to move out of orbit, speeding swiftly away . . .

Of course, we'll still stay in touch with the Bradburys. I can exchange messages for years with Barry – all my life if I want to. For he will never sleep. He will never forget.

Pen-pals through space.

Now, the ships are almost gone. Just fading sparks among the stars . . .

Goodbye, Barry. I'll miss you.

WITCH

by Brian Morse

The first time Lesley saw the wolf was the morning of her tenth birthday.

She was down by the stream, drawing a pail of water and dreaming of the presents she might have had, when she looked up and there it was, among the trees, in a pool of orange sunlight. At first her heart gave a little thump of fear and she wanted to run away. Then common sense came to her aid. She was perfectly safe. The forcefield round the homestead was switched on. Nothing could get through it.

The wolf seemed surprised too, as if it hadn't expected to be seen. It hesitated, then took a step forward. It and Lesley gazed at each other. After half a minute the wolf seemed to have seen enough. It turned and walked away. After a few steps it broke into a loping run, not frightened but as if it had an important message to deliver.

Lesley found she'd been holding her breath for a very long time. She gasped for air then hitched up her oversize trousers (Alice's cast-offs) and ran back towards the homestead as fast as her legs would take her. But at the screen between the veranda and the kitchen she pulled up short.

'You *knew* life would be hard when we got to Hope,' Marin, her foster-father, was saying. 'Was life any better on Earth? At least we've land here, a hundred square kilometres, more if we want it. What did we have on Earth? Nothing! A tiny room on floor ninety-one of block three six eight five Pacific City. The day they took us to Canaveral was the first day I'd seen the sky properly in my life, let alone grass and trees.'

'They promised a good life on Hope,' Alice, her foster-mother, sobbed. 'Not drudgery, work work work, crops failing, a winter like the Arctic, a summer like the Sahara.'

'We've had one good summer,' Marin said quickly, defensively. It had been his idea to join the colonizing expedition to Hope as Alice endlessly reminded him. 'Now they know more, the geneticists will get things right. You'll see. The seeds will be better next year. They've promised us sheep and cows when the next ship comes. Then there will be meat. They're sorting out the problems at the mine—' The mine was further up the valley. It was the reason Marin had taken a homestead in this sector. A mining engineer, he'd been promised a job underground when the copper began to be extracted. *HOPE! METAL CAPITAL OF THE UNIVERSE!* the billboards screamed at Cape Cod where the colonists disembarked.

'Home. I want to go home,' Alice sobbed. Through the place in the screen where it didn't fit quite right – Marin was a rotten carpenter and much of the homestead was already falling to pieces – Lesley could see her foster-mother rocking herself to and fro, arms clutched across her chest.

'Home! This is the only home you'll get!' Marin suddenly shouted. 'We were given a one-way ticket! Do you think they'd have brought the likes of us here otherwise? We came because anything was better than what we'd got. What did they tell us at the induction meetings? Forget Earth: you're never coming back, but work hard and you'll get rich beyond your wildest dreams!'

Suddenly Alice's tears disappeared. Her voice became harsher. 'Sheep! Cows! A decent planet would have animals that were some use to us and plants we could eat. Where's that girl gone? I sent her for water half an hour ago. If I had my way—' Alice pushed the screen open so hard it almost knocked Lesley over. 'There she is, eavesdropping again! And where's the water? What's she done with the pail?'

'I saw a wolf! It looked at me!' Lesley said. She smiled up at Alice, trying to share the pleasure the animal had given her. 'It was on the other side of the forcefield.'

'The water!' Alice screamed. 'Why haven't you brought the water? I need water! I needed it half an hour ago!'

'A wolf?' Marin said. 'You've seen a wolf? You can't have. They've classified every animal on Hope. There are no wolves. There are no animals like them. It's a peaceful planet. If there'd been wolves, they'd have killed them.'

'It just looked,' Lesley said pacifyingly. 'It didn't hurt me. I don't think it would have done anything even if the forcefield had been switched off. It looked friendly.'

What she was saying was dawning on Alice. 'She saw a wolf? I want to—' But she couldn't get out the rest.

'You little liar!' Marin shouted. 'Making things up to frighten us!' He pushed his wife aside and towered over Lesley. 'Seeing things that aren't there! You witch!'

It was the first time he'd hit her.

Until now Lesley had thought of him as her friend.

The second time Lesley saw the wolf, even if she didn't want to, was a market day. The market at Kinshasha was fifteen kilometres distant from the homestead and the track had to be walked every centimetre of the way. At first it hadn't been like that. In the first eighteen months on Hope, a hovacopter had come to collect all the people in their sector with what they had to sell from their homesteads, but the vehicle had begun breaking down. A faulty chip in the transmission, the technician who'd come from Cape Cod had said. But then hovacopters all over Hope had begun to fail, sometimes with fatal results, and it soon became clear that the manufacturers on Earth had equipped the colonists with a faulty batch. Not only that – there'd been some miscalculation when the scientists had analysed the exact composition of Hope's atmosphere, a minute mistake but enough to mean that the filters of the propulsion units were ruined too. In fact, it turned out, it had been a question of which would fail first, chips or filters.

Alice hadn't appeared at breakfast time. No explanation. All Marin said was, 'We're on our own today,' and Lesley didn't ask why. The blow in her face on her birthday two weeks before hadn't been repeated but it had taught her a lot about keeping herself to herself.

In silence she and Marin loaded the scraggy apples and potatoes they were hoping to sell on to the cart Marin had built when the hovacopter had failed for good. He hitched the ropes round his shoulders and began to pull. Lesley walked behind in the dawn light to push when they went uphill and pick up anything that fell off. As she walked she thought wistfully of how she'd loved riding the hovacopter with the people from the other homesteads, talking with her friends and gazing out at the woods and grassy slopes. Then she thought of the days at Cape Cod when their spaceship had landed on Hope. Cape Cod had been so much smarter than Kinshasha, full of the most up-to-date equipment and the bustle of astronauts and important officials all with their own transporters. They'd already been at the homestead half a year when their spaceship had disembarked for Earth. Officially another was due in five years time, but Lesley had heard settlers at the market discussing how they thought it would be much much longer before it really arrived. Of course that wasn't what Marin told Alice.

When they were about half-way Marin stopped the cart on a level piece of hillside, wedged rocks both sides of the wheels and flopped down in a piece of shade. Lesley fetched him the flask of water and a lump of bread she'd saved from breakfast. She must have gone to sleep, for the next thing she knew Marin was speaking. 'She's right really, you know, Alice is. Things should be better than this. They promised us so much, a whole new life, and it's come to this.' Lesley squinted up at him as he gestured at the cart and its pathetic load. 'At least on Earth you didn't have to walk or grub in the ground for things to eat. Hope they call it! Things can only get worse here. And the mine – I sometimes think they'll never get that going. All those problems with underground streams and lakes – they should have solved those by now. My job there—' He was silent.

For a moment Lesley thought he was going to cry. A fortnight ago she'd have put her arms round him to comfort him, for after all he wasn't a bad person, nor was Alice. It was only their unhappiness made them take things out on her. But now she just lay pretending to be asleep. That blow had changed things. It wasn't her fault she wasn't their daughter: that Alice couldn't have children of her own, that Marin and Alice as a childless couple had been forced to take her on when both her parents had died on the trip.

Above them Hope's orange sun climbed steadily into the morning sky. In Kinshasha the market would already be underway and the later they got there the less chance there'd be of selling their produce at a decent price, the less chance of buying what they needed for the coming week. If Marin wasn't going to move, she'd have to. Lesley stood up and gazed across the straggly grass towards a clump of the yellow and purple trees that were common in this part of Hope. Their fruit was almost the size of two fists put together, it looked delicious, but its taste was too bitter to stomach however hungry you were. Beneath the trees a flock of small animals – as yet they had no name – peacefully grazed. Further off at the head of the valley a thin line of smoke rose from the hidden mine buildings – the source of all Marin's dreams: a well-paid job, a better homestead, no need to play at being a farmer, the money to import his own hova-copter from Earth – the means to make Alice happy.

Lesley was about to say, 'Marin, it's time to move,' when she saw the wolf again. It was boldly making its way in the open. At first she didn't think it had seen them, but then it looked in their direction. Unlike the first time it didn't seem at all put out it had been seen. Lesley's throat went dry. She edged back, conscious that this time there was no forcefield to protect her. She stepped on Marin's foot.

'What's the matter?' Marin groggily scrambled upright. He held her shoulder. Then his voice changed. 'What are you staring at?'

'Nothing, Marin.' She pulled herself away, remembering his reaction the first time. 'Time to go.'

'Something there?' Marin was peering across the grass. 'What is it?' There was a touch of curiosity and a touch of fear in his voice. Lesley willed herself not to look.

'Nothing. You're dreaming. We've got to get to market.' Lesley had heard him telling Alice the gossip of the market last week, about a girl who'd been accused of seeing 'things', about a woman who'd defended her because she'd seen them herself, of others – men and women – in other settlements who'd claimed the same. Marin had dropped his voice when he'd told Alice about their fate. 'Witches,' he'd called them. *Witch* – it was the same word he'd used when he'd hit her.

'Something in the grass.' He wouldn't stop staring. 'Over there. What is it?' He rubbed his eyes.

'Come on, Marin. I'll help you pull.' Lesley hitched one of the straps round her shoulders. No good Marin seeing things. He'd blab, Alice would grow hysterical, they'd accuse *her* of causing it, and other people would get to know.

'Gone,' Marin said, 'Whatever it was.' He looked at Lesley dubiously.

As he took up the strain it occurred to Lesley that if Marin had seen the wolf too, if only for a moment, it must be real. Until now she'd doubted it.

'Put your back into it, girl,' Marin said.

So there were other inhabitants of Hope apart from the people from Earth and the docile herds of animals that were no good to them. Lesley dared not ask Marin what had happened to the girl and the woman who'd seen these other inhabitants. She instinctively knew it would be unpleasant.

The first time Lesley saw the wolf inside the homestead's forcefield it wasn't alone.

It was a couple of days after the trip to the market. Lesley slept in a cot in the kitchen (Alice kept the homestead's second bedroom for the child she would never have) and that night Lesley woke as if a bolt of electricity had gone through her. Three wolves were by the door, two squatting on their haunches, the one she'd seen before inspecting a piece of electrical equipment Marin had not even bothered to put a plug on since the solar panels they'd been issued with didn't function as efficiently in Hope's atmosphere as Earth's (another of the scientists' miscalculations). She was about to scream but it was as if the leading wolf had put a finger across her lips. She couldn't scream and then she didn't want to. They didn't mean any harm.

But when they'd gone Lesley would have liked to have run in to Alice and Marin for comfort – not because the wolves had threatened her in any way but because of their alien-ness. They'd been different from the wolves in the old life nature micro-videos they'd shown the children on the ship or the wolves in stories. They'd been stronger, deeper, more intelligent. More than that, the wolves had communicated, not with Lesley but with each other as they'd systematically checked through the contents of the kitchen – not talk-communication like humans but by some method of their own. Lesley lay where she was. On the way back from the market Marin had told her exactly what had happened to others who'd seen them. She realized it had been his way of protecting her, but it had also been his way of threatening her to keep quiet, of not bringing trouble to his home. The girl in Kinshasha had been beaten to within inches of her life by angry homesteaders. The woman had only escaped being burnt to death by escaping from the settlement. No-one knew where she'd gone. If they had they'd have followed her. They'd have followed her, Marin had emphasized, and burnt her. It was what you did to witches – people who had truck with the devil, the people to blame for the ills that were beginning to afflict Hope. She had no right to see what wasn't there. No-one had. That only frightens people.

Lesley came back from the stream with the pail of water. She dumped it on the porch and listened. Marin was telling Alice the truth – Lesley had heard him building up to it over the last few days. It was now official – there'd be no more spaceships from Earth. A message had come through. The people of Hope had been abandoned. Since they'd left Earth there'd been a terrible war, famine and plague had followed, and the homesteaders and the officials at Cape Cod had been lucky to get away. Life on Hope – even if the crops failed, even if the native fruits and animals were useless as food, even if the hovacopters and half the other machines they'd brought from Earth had broken down – was infinitely better than that on Earth at that moment.

Lucky. Alice didn't think she was lucky!

Marin hadn't told her what else the news meant. That there was no point to Hope now. The copper mine at the head of the valley, all the other hundreds of mines on Hope, would have no customers.

The colonists might as well not have come.

Lesley sat on the crumbling edge of the porch and gazed back towards the stream. She waited for Marin to calm Alice down. It would take hours this time.

Lesley could understand Alice's upset, but somehow she couldn't share it. Perhaps it was because Hope was the only planet she'd known, the only future she'd ever had. She loved Hope with its orange sun and vivid colours. She didn't care what it had been like on Earth. She'd seen how beautiful it was on the micro-videos but it wasn't her planet. It never would be.

And then there were the wolves. She wasn't afraid of them, even if they'd kept themselves hidden till now. She welcomed them, as if making contact with them might make Hope live up to its name.

She shivered as the breeze plucked at her clothes. Beyond the stream the wind was beginning to buffet the treetops. High above, clouds were beginning to fill the sky. Rain tonight.

The weather woke Lesley in the early hours of the morning. Wind and rain were rocking the homestead, the kitchen door banging to and fro on its latch. A window in the living-room Marin used as a makeshift workshop sounded as if it had managed to work itself completely loose. Every other gust pulled at the flimsy homestead roof and threatened to lift it off altogether.

Lesley loved storms. She wriggled out from under her blanket and pulled aside the curtain at the kitchen window. As she pressed her face to the glass a bolt of lightning screeched across the sky and struck deep among the woods on the hillside beyond the stream. There were flames as the lightning set a tree alight but to her disappointment the blaze went out straightaway. The crack of thunder was almost above the homestead. Lesley clapped her hands to her ears.

She was turning back to fetch the blanket to wrap round her when she realized the rain and the lightning hadn't been the only things out there. Something had been moving among Marin's vegetable patches and rows of stunted apple trees. Something? What? What could have got past the forcefield? She rubbed at the window where her breath had steamed it up.

Another flash creased the sky. This time the bolt of lightning struck even closer. In the white light that filled the familiar landscape, in the eerie moment before the thunder cracked, she saw the homestead garden and orchard and all the ground towards the stream was alive with creatures – not just wolves, though they were there too, but other creatures, serpent-like, dragon-like creatures, creatures she could not begin to describe to herself, a stream of them jostling and flowing towards the window at which she was standing. She began to scream, to warn Marin and Alice, but the lightning flashed again and

47

Lesley saw the stream of creatures was dividing as it reached the house and flowing past it, and that the creatures weren't interested in her or her foster-parents. They were fleeing something.

'Alice! Marin!' She burst into their room. They were sitting up in bed. Marin's arms were round Alice, protecting her. Alice had her face buried deep in Marin's chest.

Marin tried to wave Lesley away, but this was no time for worrying about obedience and the way Alice thought foster-daughters ought to behave. 'We've got to leave!' she shouted. Marin stared at her without understanding. 'Something's happening, some disaster.'

'The storm will blow itself out. They always do,' Marin mumbled. He turned his face to the bedroom window which at that moment was a sheet of hot white. 'Go back to bed, girl.' He freed a hand and pointed a finger at Alice, warning Lesley. Alice clung even more closely to him.

'This one won't!' Lesley shouted. Marin shook his head at her, bewildered by her insistence. 'Look out of the window if you don't believe me!' She pulled at the bedclothes and wrenched them off and pulled at Alice who was trembling with fright. 'Dress her!' she shouted at Marin. Marin was trembling too. She glanced out of the window. The stream of creatures was a torrent now. 'Marin! Do as you're told!'

Her foster-father began to obey her.

∗   ∗   ∗

How they could not see them Lesley could not understand as she guided Marin and Alice away from the homestead towards higher ground. Alice seemed to stumble at every other step. Marin kept turning back to stare in the direction of the homestead. Every time the thunder cracked he flinched.

At last they reached higher ground. Lesley found shelter under a rock. The creatures flowed past.

At last no more came except a wolf that stopped and stood a few metres away. Alice and Marin huddled closer together, but it seemed to Lesley that the wolf smiled at her. It was as if she'd passed a test.

'All my work ruined!' Marin poked among the mud-streaked wreckage of the homestead scattered across where the orchard and vegetable patch had been. The flood that had destroyed it had carried down the buildings from the copper mine further up the valley, and torn its machinery out of the bowels of the earth. A great metal beam pinned down Marin's shattered cart on the bank of the stream. Even if Earth had been waiting for the copper the mine wouldn't have been able to supply it now. 'What shall we do? Where shall we go?' Lesley tried to think of comforting words, but they didn't come. Alice, on the other hand, seemed almost pleased it had happened, as if it meant she could go back to Earth.

'How did you know, Lesley? How could you have

told?' Marin had already asked her a dozen times. He thrust his face up close. 'How did you know it was going to happen? You did know, didn't you? You knew. Who told you? Tell me.'

Something in Lesley snapped. 'I saw them out of the window. There were hundreds of creatures. They knew what was going to happen. I followed them.'

'Saw them?'

'Wolves, dragons, serpents. I don't know what they're all called. They were all around you as we climbed the hill. Surely you saw them!'

'Hope is a safe planet. There are no wolves,' Marin said dully. 'Hope's evolutionary pattern has eliminated all dangerous animals.' It was as if he was quoting from an official handout. He swung away from Lesley, then back again. He'd been working up to this. '*Witch!*' he said. 'We've been harbouring a witch all this time. Devil's brat! Without you and your sort none of this would have happened!'

'Witch!' Alice echoed him. She pointed a finger at Lesley. The way she did it seemed witch-like itself.

'You saw a wolf yourself when we were on the way to the market!' Lesley shouted. 'Yes, you did, Marin! You saw it! Admit the truth! You know we're not the only intelligent creatures who live here and that scares you! It scares you to death!'

Marin swung back. His fist was raised. 'No-one says that to me!' He stepped towards her.

★   ★   ★

51

Lesley sat in the sun on the rock that had sheltered them during the worst of the storm. The woman who'd disappeared and the girl the woman had stood up for – they and all the others like them, that was who she needed to find. Even if that meant abandoning her foster-parents, she needed to be with people who understood – with people who weren't afraid of the truth about Hope, who knew that they'd only scratched its surface appearance, that there were other inhabitants they needed to make contact with if they wanted to survive. She'd no doubt that at this very moment Marin and Alice would be telling the neighbouring homesteaders that the foster-child the authorities had foisted on them had turned out to be a witch, a child of the devil. A search party would be being organized. If the choice was between hunting her down in vengeance or picking up the pieces and beginning again, she knew which one they'd make. Earth people were like that.

But she wasn't an Earth person. She was a child of Hope.

She got up to walk.

Which way?

A wolf, the wolf that had been down by the stream and in the kitchen, was standing close to her. *That way, Lesley*, it said. Her head hurt as its voice for the first time spoke in her mind. *That way, Lesley. You'll find the people you seek that way. There are others of us on your journey who will help you. Welcome to Hope.*

THE BLUBBLE
by Douglas Hill

Cal was in the water, playing with the silkies, when the alert siren sounded. Quickly looking over at the Barge, he saw the hover-flare spinning above it. The livid blue flare of a monster alert.

Treading water, he stared nervously around. But then he relaxed. It was only a blubble, some distance away, slow-moving and unthreatening.

Blubbles were the biggest creatures in that alien ocean, looming out of the water as big as houses – if houses could be great shapeless domes of puffy, bulgy flesh. Some of the crew of the Barge thought they looked like blobs, some said more like bubbles. So they were called blubbles.

They seemed to have no eyes or ears or anything, other than a great many long ropy tentacles dangling

53

from the underside. They also seemed to have no real brain to speak of. They just drifted aimlessly, in large numbers – this one was the fourth Cal had seen that day – showing no interest in the humans who tried to examine them.

Floating calmly, Cal watched the huge ballooning shape drift nearer. He was supposed to return at once to the Barge during an alert, for no-one ever took chances, not even with blubbles. But he was in no hurry. And the blubble was moving past him, anyway, towards a large floating spread of edible greenweed – the dense growth that was food for many of the life-forms on that planet.

The planet was named Talirre, and was an ocean planet, with only a small scattering of islands dotted over its vast surface. And Cal was the youngest member of an exploration team from Earth, working on their 'Project' – a full study of Talirre's ocean and its creatures.

At the age of eleven, Cal was well below the minimum age for such a team. But his parents were famous marine scientists, experts on alien oceans. The Project had wanted them, so it had to have Cal as well.

The team's base, called the Barge, was in fact a special kind of space shuttle. It had brought the team down to Talirre from the giant starship that stayed in orbit around the planet. On water, the shuttle could be transformed into an enormous floating vessel, as long as three football fields. Where the Project team had been living and working for several months.

In that time they had learned a great deal about the dark, warm, peaceful, alien ocean of Talirre. They had solved some of its mysteries, and were working hard to solve others. They were all having a fine time. And so was Cal, though he had little work to do.

With the Barge's scanners keeping a non-stop watch on the ocean, Cal was given a good deal of freedom. He was the best swimmer on the Barge – everyone knew that. And, anyway, swimming in that ocean was so easy. The water was full of minerals, harmless but dark-coloured, which made the water cloudy and murky but also made it amazingly buoyant. A swimmer could stay afloat with very little effort.

So Cal spent much of every day in the water, swimming with the silkies. They were small, sleekly furry creatures who had appeared around the Barge when it first landed, and who visited it often, filled with playful curiosity. Anyone going swimming from the Barge ended up playing with the silkies, who were as swift and agile in the water as otters. As swimmers, they made even Cal look slow and clumsy. At times, indeed, he felt that their merry hoots and squeaks sounded as if they were laughing at him.

He was still floating, watching the blubble, when the alert siren shrieked again. He jumped guiltily, thinking it had been sounded especially for him, because he hadn't started to swim back.

'I'm coming, I'm coming,' he muttered aloud.

But then he realized that the second siren wasn't just for him. He saw a fiery *red* hover-flare going up to spin next to the blue one. A *storm* alert, as well as a monster alert.

And beyond the Barge, he saw the gathering cloud-shapes of one of Talirre's incredible hurricane-storms, which could toss even the enormous Barge around as if it was a dinghy.

Already the wind was getting up, stirring the water into great heaves that would soon become mighty foaming waves like mountains. Cal saw the blubble starting to sink below the surface, where most ocean creatures went on Talirre during a storm. The silkies, too, were swimming rapidly away – before diving beneath the surface and vanishing.

Where do they go? Cal wondered, for perhaps the thousandth time. It was one of the unsolved mysteries of Talirre. The silkies were *air*-breathing water creatures, like otters or seals on Earth. Yet there was almost no land where they could rest or seek shelter. During storms, they seemed to vanish under-water. But then – why didn't they drown?

Puzzling over the alien strangeness, Cal began to swim home. But he stopped when he glimpsed a movement nearby. Something had bobbed up out of the water in the midst of the floating raft of green-weed.

It was another swimmer, he saw. A tiny, slender woman in a full wetsuit, with a flexi-helmet that had its own small air supply. It's Doctor Anja, Cal realized. Out in the weed as usual.

Doctor Anja was a brilliant scientist who was the head of the whole Project. She was also a lively, energetic woman who was especially interested in the greenweed and the creatures that ate it. Though not a very good swimmer, she spent every spare moment in the water, studying the weed.

And she could be a bit absent-minded, Cal knew, when she was busy. She probably hadn't even noticed the alert flares. So he turned and swam towards her.

Doctor Anja opened her face-plate, smiled and waved. 'Hello, Cal,' she called cheerily. 'All by yourself? No silkies?'

'They've gone, Doctor,' Cal said. 'There's a storm alert.'

She looked at the Barge and blinked, surprised. 'So there is.'

Cal glanced uneasily around at the waves, which were growing larger. 'We'd better hurry back,' he said.

'In a moment,' Doctor Anja said. 'My helmet has a bit of air left, so I'll just make one more dive. I need a sample from underneath the weed.' And she closed her face-plate and sank below the surface.

Cal waited where he was, treading water. Moments passed, then more. The waves were getting a lot bigger, he thought nervously, but he didn't want to leave Doctor Anja. She was quite capable of forgetting all about the alert until the full fury of the storm came down upon her.

More moments passed, and Cal grew more anxious. Doctor Anja had said she had only 'a bit' of air left. How could she stay down so long? What if something had gone wrong?

He suddenly felt cold despite the water's warmth. It would be unbearable if something happened to Doctor Anja. She was kind and friendly, and she was also the most important person on the Barge. She just couldn't be *lost* or anything . . .

Even as he thought those thoughts, Cal was diving – spearing down through the dark water. He could see nothing in the murkiness, but he had to try to find the doctor. He had to try . . .

And then something like a long, rough, sinewy rope snaked out of the depths, wrapped around his middle, and dragged him down.

He fought wildly, kicking and flailing. But he could not break free. And his panicky struggle quickly used up the gulp of air he had taken. As he was pulled farther down, a roaring began in his ears, a blazing pain in his chest. He sagged, weakening, sure that he was drowning.

In that instant the rope-thing brought him up against something solid. As he touched it, it seemed to open before him, as a mouth opens. Sea water rushed through the opening, carrying Cal with it. He landed with a thump on a wet but solid surface – and found that he could breathe.

The air was warm and thick, with a foul stink like nothing he had ever known. Yet it was air. Unless, he thought dazedly, it was a final dream, while he drowned. But he didn't think so. He had never had a dream that *stank*.

He stared around, amazed that he could see as well as breathe. He was in a weird sort of chamber, with uneven floor and walls and ceiling that looked somehow rubbery. On the walls he saw broad smears of stuff that he thought might be some kind of mould, for that was where the light came from – a feeble glow that some moulds can produce. Getting to his feet, he peered into the shadows along the walls, looking for the opening that had let him in.

And something moved in those shadows.

He stumbled back with a gasp, panic clawing at him again. Until he heard the soft hoots and squeaks, very familiar sounds. As his eyes grew more used to the dimness, he saw the shapes in the shadows more clearly, and sighed with relief.

Silkies. Probably the very ones he had been playing with, before.

He stepped forward over the floor of the chamber, where quite a lot of water was scattered in separate pools here and there. Then he glanced down at the nearest pool – and stiffened with another icy surge of shock.

Something was lying in that pool. Something with a human shape, in a wetsuit, with a helmet.

Doctor Anja. Lying face down in the water, unmoving.

Frantically Cal reached for her, pulling her up, while the silkies squeaked nervously at the sudden splashing. Luckily the doctor was small, and Cal could easily drag her limp form out into the air, on her back. He yanked open the helmet's face-plate, praying that she would be alive.

For a long terrible second she did not move. Then she jerked, with a weak cough, water dribbling from her lips. And she began to breathe.

She was still unconscious, but she was alive. Cal sighed again, kneeling beside her. Probably the same thing that got me got her, he thought. But what was it? The Project had never found any creatures on Talirre with long, ropy tentacles like the one that had grabbed him. Except . . .

His eyes widened as the answer came to him.

The blubble.

Blubbles had lots of tentacles. And there had been a blubble there, underwater.

He stared around unbelievingly, remembering how he had been dragged down and forced through the strange opening like a mouth. That must be it, he thought. He was inside the blubble. As if the giant

creature had *eaten* him – and Doctor Anja, and the silkies.

But he wasn't being *digested* or anything. And the silkies weren't behaving like creatures that had been caught and eaten. In fact, as he looked at them again, he realized that it was the *silkies* who were doing the eating.

Their deft little paws were busily scraping the luminous mould from the walls of the chamber. Then they were stuffing the mould into their mouths, gobbling it as if it was the tastiest delicacy in the galaxy.

Again Cal recognized what he was seeing. He was, after all, the son of two marine scientists, and he knew a bit about how things worked in nature. Even alien nature.

The blubble and the silkies were doing favours for one another. The blubble offered the little air-breathers a safe underwater haven during one of the ocean's titanic storms. In turn, the silkies 'cleaned' the mould off the inside walls of the blubble's stomach, or whatever it was.

Cal even knew the scientific word for when two very different kinds of creature help each other in that sort of way. *Symbiosis*, it was called.

Probably, he guessed, the silkies can't see underwater any better than I can. So when a storm starts they just swim in the general direction of the nearest blubble. And somehow it senses them, grabs them and brings them into its air chamber.

Only this time it brought a couple of humans, too.

He grinned to himself. Everyone on the Project would be amazed at how he had solved the mystery of where the silkies went, underwater. He might be able to help set up monitors and things, to find out if blubbles *always* came to the silkies when a storm threatened. He sat back, still grinning, thinking about it.

But some while later, his grin had entirely faded.

He had no idea how long it had been – but long enough. And nothing had happened in that time. Above all, there had been no hint at all of when, or how, they would be able to get out.

Surely the silkies would have a way out, somehow, sometime. But *when*? By then most of the silkies had curled up on the floor and gone to sleep, as if content to stay there for *days*. By which time he and Doctor Anja might either starve, or have to risk eating the alien mould.

But there was a more immediate worry. Doctor Anja was still unconscious, hardly having moved except for a twitch or two. Cal couldn't even see her clearly, since the dimness was worse after the silkies had eaten a lot of the glowing mould. But he was growing very frightened for her. What if she had been *damaged* somehow, by those moments without air? What if she was *dying*? What if . . .

His mind spun off into other terrifying directions.

Worst of all, there was nothing he could do. Not while he was helplessly trapped inside an alien monster, deep under an alien sea . . .

Then he jumped as if he had been stabbed – as a shaky voice spoke his name. 'Cal . . . ?'

Doctor Anja was gazing up at him, wide-eyed with astonishment.

'Doctor, you're *alive*!' Cal gasped.

She struggled weakly to sit up. 'So it seems,' she said. 'I just remember something grabbing me . . .' Her voice trembled with the memory of terror. 'Did you save me, Cal?'

'Not exactly,' Cal said, fumbling. 'Or . . . maybe. Sort of.'

She stared at him, mystified, then peered around. 'I don't understand. Where are we? And what's that *stink*?'

Cal took a deep breath. 'It's . . . really an amazing thing . . .'

Then he stopped. Because something on one wall, which had seemed to be only a fold in the rubbery surface, suddenly began to pull apart. Like a valve, or a mouth, opening.

And a rush of dark ocean water flooded in upon them like a mighty tide.

Once again Cal was fighting, panic-stricken, for his life. But not alone, this time. As that sudden flood of water struck, he had grabbed Doctor Anja's hand.

Clutching it as tightly as he could, dragging her with him, he kicked and thrashed, trying to swim in the blinding darkness, trying to find a surface, to reach the air. The water surged over the two of them, flinging them around in a powerful current, whirling them forward. Struggling helplessly, with no idea where he was or where the air-chamber was, Cal fought on, clinging to the doctor. And again a roaring grew in his ears, pain filled his air-starved chest . . .

Until all at once he saw a vast brightness above him. And with a desperate kick and lunge his head popped up above the surface of the ocean.

He took a huge breath of the most wonderful air he had ever breathed, pulling Doctor Anja up in the buoyant water so she could also breathe. And as she coughed and spluttered and gasped, Cal stared around at a scene of furious, total madness.

The storm was over, the sky was clear, the sea was calm again. Except at one place, where the water was being churned up by just about every smaller vessel from the Barge. As flyers circled overhead, all the boats – skimmers, drifters, watersleds and more – zipped and swirled around on the water, while mini-subs and swimmers in powered wetsuits rose and fell in repeated dives underwater. All of them were moving at speed, perhaps in some pattern, but looking frenzied and crazed.

They're *searching*, Cal realized. For Doctor Anja – and me.

He heard a squeaking behind him, and turned, still floating easily, to see the silkies swimming quickly away from all the human madness. Beyond them, he saw the vast puffy shape of the blubble, also drifting away.

It'll really be interesting, Cal thought, to find out exactly how it works – the symbiosis between the blubble and the silkies. But there would be time for that, once things got back to normal. As they seemed about to do – for one of the flyers had spotted Cal and the doctor where they floated.

At once the whole armada of machines turned and hurtled towards them. And Cal spotted his mother and father, looking pale and frantic, in one of the skimmers at the front.

He lifted an arm in a great happy wave. And Doctor Anja, still supported by his other arm, peered blearily at him.

'Cal . . .' she croaked. 'You *did* save me, didn't you?'

'I suppose so, sort of,' Cal agreed, still waving. Then he grinned. 'But you know what *else*? I found out where the silkies go in storms!'

SKYJACKED
by Mary Hoffman

Trel looked up from the console and stretched her shoulders till they cracked. It had been a long day. First navigating the meteor shower, then dealing with a laser rocket attack while half the ship's defence systems were down, and finally that last manoeuvre to avoid being sucked into a black hole. She flexed her fingers and glanced back up at the viewscreen. 'What now?' A row of brilliant white fire-flashes was approaching. 'Disintegrating ship? Comet? Kamikaze attack?'

The doors to the flight deck swooshed open and a sandy-haired boy a bit older than Trel burst in.

'Message from Commander Arcturus,' he barked. 'You're to get off that simulator at once!'

'Zawn!' objected Trel. 'Just look at that screen.

I've never had one of those – it would be a real challenge.'

'But Arcturus says there are other students who need the practice and you've missed two lectures.'

Trel snorted. 'Yeah, Suspended Animation and Android Programming. I don't want to know all that, Zawn. I want to practise flying. Well, really I want to fly – not practise – but you know what they're like here.'

Zawn looked pointedly at the console and Trel sighed and switched off the red button. The bright white lights faded from the screen, for ever unidentified and were replaced by a sign:

THANK YOU FOR FLYING SIMILNAV.
HAVE A NICE DAY!

Trel scowled at it. 'What else did my uncle say?'

'He said if you keep disobeying Academy rules and designing your own curriculum, when you graduate. *if* you graduate, he'll make sure you fly your first mission in a CrapZapper.'

'Sounds as if he's in a mood,' said Trel, walking out with Zawn. As the doors swished closed, the students stepped down into the sprawling Academy complex, leaving the squat white simulator behind them.

Trel sighed again. 'You'd think it would help

having your uncle in charge of this place, wouldn't you?'

Zawn shrugged. 'How would I know? I don't even know if I've got an uncle, let alone who he is.'

Trel got as close to blushing as she ever did. Just for a minute she'd forgotten about Zawn's background. Like most students, she was the child of a normal three-parent family. But Zawn was a Tuggaluv, a scholarship boy – just as brilliant a pilot as Trel but, unlike her, not knowing where he got it from. She punched his arm.

'Whoever he is, I bet he's an alpha starship captain,' she said. 'Come on, I'll buy you a Millenium Shake before we go back to class.'

They linked arms and walked over to the nutriteria. Beyond the complex, Trel noticed an ungainly red and silver ship docking at the spaceport. It reminded her of Uncle Arky's threat. He'd never let his own niece fly a bucket like that, surely? Not while his sister's the captain of the best ship in the squadron?

They watched the clumsy CrapZapper complete its awkward manoeuvre. Cosmic Retrieval and Anti-Pollution vehicles had been re-named in a recent public relations drive to improve their image. But they were still the garbage disposal units of the twenty-fifth century, cleaning up the mess of five hundred years of space exploration. Bits of satellites, defunct probes, jettisoned rocket boosters from as far back as the twentieth century when space had still seemed infinite; all had to be brought back or destroyed by someone, or they presented hazards for today's spaceships.

Their pilots were the Academy drop-outs or failed finalists, who had scraped enough knowhow and flying hours to get a Limited Licence. That was all you needed for a Zapper. Not the kind of ship a star pupil wanted for her first mission.

They sat and drank their shakes. 'When's your dad due back?' asked Zawn.

'A week or two,' said Trel, frowning. She had better watch herself or the commander would send a bad report of her to Ambassador Fullbright. Her diplomat father was much more alarming to her than her brilliant commanding mother was. She didn't feel she had a diplomatic gene in her system; she might as well have been cloned as bio-gotten.

Her frown deepened as two red and silver clad pilots came into the nutriteria and punched their orders into the wall.

'What are they doing in here?' she hissed.

'Getting a drink is what it looks like,' said Zawn.

'But they aren't allowed on to the complex. How'd they get past the security?'

'Like this, kiddo,' said the taller pilot, drawing a stun-gun from his jerkin.

The other one took out a small device that looked like a bio-corder of some sort and scanned the two students with it. 'Bingo!' he said with an evil grin. 'We don't have to search the place after all.'

There was no-one around to help. All orders were dealt with by machines and the rest of the students were in class or lectures. Trel and Zawn were unarmed and helpless. The Zapper pilots bundled them off to the complex and into the spaceport where their craft waited.

'OK,' said the tall one. 'We're going to call your father and you're going to tell him that you're safe, but if he ever wants to see you alive again he'd better come back to Earth by the next shuttle.'

'He won't do that!' shouted Trel. 'He's in the middle of important negotiations with the Minervans.'

'Who asked you, half-pint?' said the other one, thrusting his sarcastic grin right into her face. 'Let your big brother do the talking.'

There was a stunned silence. Trel heard her voice crack as she said, 'You've made a big mistake. Zawn's not my brother. I'm Ambassador Fullbright's only child.'

'Tell her, Trader,' said the tall one, smiling.

Trader took out the electronic device again. 'You seen one of these? No? It seems you Academy types don't know everything then. It's a DNA decoder. We fed in the DNA codes of Captain and Ambassador Fullbright and it told Mink and me which individuals have the personal codes that could come from them and only them. Neat, huh?'

'Mind you,' said Mink, 'we were only expecting one.'

Trel was fighting back tears. Something huge and frightening was happening, something worse than being kidnapped. 'There is only one,' she gasped. 'Me.'

Zawn, who had said nothing since their capture, slowly turned to look at her. Their eyes met, the same colour, in an identical glance of understanding. 'It could be, Trel,' he said. 'Remember I don't know who my bio-parents were.'

The Zapper pilots goggled, then burst into guffaws of laughter.

'Aah,' said Trader, mockingly. 'Diddums doesn't know his mummy and daddy!'

'Poor little Tuggaluv,' added Mink.

Trel just looked at Zawn in amazement. Her parents had never said that they had tried to have a child before her. It was routine for high-ranking Star Council officials, both in the Space Squadron and the Diplomatic Corps, to use surrogate mothers. The procedure normally went smoothly, but just occasionally the mothers who gave birth to the children refused to hand them over. There were courts to decide on such cases, but if the surrogate could prove she was in danger of mental breakdown if 'her' child was removed, she was allowed to keep it.

Such children, the Tuggaluvs, were heavily disadvantaged, being brought up by only one parent, instead of three, but they could and often did win Academy scholarships, like Zawn.

'Do you think it could be true, Zawn?' Trel whispered.

He nodded. 'You remember your first day at the Academy, when those kids were ragging you about your uncle?'

Trel remembered. Zawn had waded in, all elbows and knees to disperse the crowd of bullies. He had been her friend and protector ever since, as well as the best student there. He had been just like a big brother in fact.

Trel gave a snort that was halfway between a sob and a giggle. 'He's your uncle too, then!'

And suddenly it didn't matter that she and her best friend, her brother, were held hostage by desperate space terrorists.

The Zapper pilots eyed the grinning pair suspiciously.

'We'd better use the girl first,' said Mink, 'if Fullbright doesn't know he's got a son.'

'Yeah,' said Trader. 'We'll keep that little surprise for later. But let's put some distance between us and that Academy first. Tie them up, Mink.'

It seemed like days later but could only have been a couple of hours. The CrapZapper was out in deep space, its captives bound and in a dark hold. Trel had sent the video-message to her father, with a laser-gun at her back. She had hated saying every word of it. She knew her father loved her, just as she knew her mother did and her Matoo, who had given birth to her and looked after her since she was a baby. But she knew how important her father's work was. If he left Minerva now, the whole sector could de-stabilize and there could be war between the Minervans and their neighbours, the Bacchae. Who would want that?

'Are you awake, Zawn?' she whispered.

'Yes,' came his low voice. 'I've got too much on my mind for sleep.'

'I've been thinking. Why would anyone want to get my, I mean, our father off Minerva? Someone must be paying those two clowns big starbucks to risk arrest for kidnapping and treason.'

'It has to be someone working for the Bacchic government, I suppose.'

'But why should they want war?'

'I don't know, but if you study the history of any galaxy, whenever peace talks were sabotaged, it was because one side wanted war.'

'We've got to stop it,' said Trel firmly. 'I'm not having any history-hologram of Minerva saying war with Bacchus started because of Astrella Fullbright!'

Zawn laughed. 'I think that's what's called de-lusions of grandeur. No-one will ever know why the peace talks broke up.'

'Then we just have to make sure they don't.'

'OK, hero–sister, what's the plan?'

Trel thought hard. 'Did you go to that lecture on suspended animation?'

'Sure. I *never* bunk lectures.'

'OK, OK, don't rub it in. Could you do it, here and now?'

'I suppose so,' said Zawn slowly. 'I've got the demo-pack. I was on my way back from the lecture when I fetched you out of the simulator.'

'Can you control it? I mean, could you do it for twenty minutes or so?'

'Yes, that bit's easy. What's the idea?'

'And could you teach me how to do it to someone else?' Trel persisted.

'Ye-es. Oh, I think I'm beginning to see. But we've got to get my right hand free.'

'What's that racket?' asked Trader.

'Sounds like our little princess,' grinned Mink. 'I'd better go and see what's upsetting her highness.'

The yelling got louder and louder as he worked his way back to the hold. By the time he got there, Trel was red in the face from shouting and looked genuinely upset. Zawn was deathly quiet.

'What's the matter?' asked Mink. He didn't like the look of it.

'It's Zawn,' gasped Trel. 'There's something wrong. He . . . he just sort of collapsed.'

Mink was on his knees, untying Zawn's bonds in

such a hurry that he didn't notice one was a bit loose. 'Is he sick or something? Has he ever done this before?'

'He's . . . delicate,' said Trel. 'If you untie me too, I can do a reading with my bio-corder.'

'Just tell me where it is.'

'You wouldn't be able to use it; it's very advanced. It took me months to learn.' Trel was banking on Mink having dropped out long before bio-cording or suspended animation occurred in the Academy syllabus. She was relieved it wasn't Trader who had come in response to her screams; he seemed a lot cleverer than Mink.

After some grumbling, Mink released her arms, leaving her legs tied. Trel whipped out a calculator, waved it over Zawn and punched a few buttons.

She showed Mink a string of equations on the display. 'See?' she said. 'Vital signs very faint. He could be dying. We've got to get medical help straightaway.'

Mink peered at the figures, which were actually a calculation of the light years between Earth and Minerva.

'Yeah,' he said doubtfully. 'I can see that. But what can we do? We don't carry medical-droids on short-haul zapping trips.'

'You'll have to get Trader to make for the nearest spaceport.'

'Most likely Trader will just chuck him off the ship,' said Mink gloomily.

Trel froze in real horror.

'I'm sorry, but you told us yourself that your dad doesn't know about him. We're only being paid to hold one kid and get the ambassador off Minerva. No-one knows about this one.'

Trel thought fast. 'I know about him. And I'm not going to keep quiet. Do you think Trader will throw me out of the ship as well? I'm no good as a hostage unless I'm alive you know.'

Mink thought about this one. And while he was distracted, Trel gingerly drew out the syringe Zawn had given her. There was a hiss as the blood-chilling serum went into his body, and Mink slumped to the ground.

Trel removed her leg-bonds and tied Mink's ankles with them. Then she bound his hands and rolled him to the far end of the hold.

'One down and one to go,' she mused grimly, rubbing her own wrists to get the circulation going again. 'Hurry up, Zawn, you should be coming round soon. I don't want to tackle Trader on my own.'

Back on the flight deck, Trader was puzzled by what was keeping Mink so long. He handed over to the standby pilot, a flying and navigation droid, and went to the back of the ship.

'What the . . . ?' was as far as he got before hearing

a sharp hiss and seeing his own personal galaxy of stars.

'Sleep well,' said Zawn, looking down at the two pilots, neatly trussed up.

'Will they be all right?' asked Trel. 'They look awfully, you know, dead.'

'They're supposed to. That's what suspended animation's like. They'll come round in a couple of hours.'

'What's it feel like?' asked Trel.

'Horrible,' said Zawn, cheerfully. 'Just like being dead, I imagine. But the waking up's great. Come on then, let's see if we can fly this bucket.'

Trel made straight for the pilot's seat, cracking her knuckles with excitement, only to find a sonic barrier preventing her access. The AutoNaut seated in the co-pilot's chair turned a silver head towards her.

'SOR–RY,' said a mechanical voice. 'ON–LY OP–ER–A–TIVES TRA–DER AND MINK AL–LOWED TO O–VER–RIDE.'

Trel was furious, but Zawn began to laugh. 'You really shouldn't bunk lectures, sister dear,' he said.

Trel groaned and pounded her head with both fists. 'Android Programming!'

'But fortunately for you, your brother took copious notes.' Zawn took out his electronic notebook and refreshed his memory. He looked round the sparsely-equipped cabin and took down a gadget

79

hooked on the wall. 'This is a pilot's remote. I'll try it.' He activated the beam.

'COP-Y CAP-TAIN TRA-DER,' said the droid.

Zawn clasped his hands above his head in victory.

'CON-FIRM I-D WITH CODE NAME,' remarked the droid pleasantly.

Zawn lowered his arms again. 'Er, um,' he said.

'IN-COR-RECT,' said the droid. 'CON-FIRM I-D.'

Trel had an inspiration. 'BACCHUS!' she yelled.

'COR-RECT,' said the droid, de-activating the barrier. 'WILL YOU BE NEED-ING MY SER-VIC-ES AS BACK-UP?'

'No,' said Zawn hastily. 'Let's quit while we're ahead.' After jabbing a few buttons on the remote, he got the droid to close down. 'Phew,' he said. 'That was a close one. If we hadn't got the barrier down, this Zapper would have flown straight on whatever course Trader had set till the fuel ran out!'

Trel slipped into the pilot's seat and Zawn lifted the droid out of the co-pilot's place.

'That was an inspiration about Bacchus,' he said.

'Yeah,' said Trel grimly, studying the controls. 'I wonder what Mink calls himself. They're obviously both in the pay of the Bacchae. Now, where shall we go?'

'Hang on,' said Zawn. 'Hadn't you better contact the ambassador first? Maybe we can stop him leaving Minerva.'

But it was no good. Councillors on Minerva gave

them the co-ordinates of the ambassador's own ship, which was already on course for Earth. They praised Trel for her escape but she cut them off. 'No time to lose,' she said. 'We've got to get to them before they make the jump into light space, or we'll waste precious hours.'

'That means we have to make the jump ourselves,' objected Zawn. 'Are you sure you can do that?'

'Sure?' said Trel. 'Sure. I've done it dozens of times.'

'Only on a simulator.'

'There has to be a first time it's for real for any pilot.'

'Yes, but for two kids in a CrapZapper?'

'Here goes nothing,' said Trel, her fingers flickering rapidly over the console. 'Hold on to your breakfast!'

Jumping light felt a bit like coming out of suspended animation, a rushing of sounds and flashes of light closing in a tunnel which suddenly burst open again into calm, star-filled space.

'Wow!' said Zawn. 'You did it!'

Trel was feeling shaky but pleased with herself. 'Lay in a course for Dad's ship, brother,' she said. 'He's in for the surprise of his life.'

Ambassador Fullbright, pacing anxiously up and down the bridge of the Starship Ventura, was surprised enough to be hailed by what appeared on screen to be a Cosmic Retrieval and Anti-Pollution vehicle. When he recognized the captain's voice, he was amazed. But when the Zapper's landing pod docked and disgorged *two* Academy students he felt the need to sit down with a long, stiff drink.

'So you see,' persisted Trel. 'If you turn the ship straight back now, the talks won't be sabotaged. It all depends on you. And do get someone to fetch those garbage clowns over. I imagine they will have some interesting stories to tell when they come round. There's a perfectly good AutoNaut too.'

'Right,' said the ambassador, snapping back into his most formal manner. 'Lay in a new course for Minerva, Ensign. And CO, please get me Captain Fullbright's ship and then Commander Arcturus on Earth.' He turned. 'And what about your parents, young man? Shouldn't we let them know you're safe?'

Zawn was saved from answering this one by the face of Captain Andromeda Fullbright filling the viewscreen with her relief and anxiety.

When she had gone, her place was taken by Commander Arcturus.

'Trel!' he barked.

'Yessir!' said Trel, jumping to attention.

'What did I tell you about missing lectures?'

'That I'd fly my first mission in a Zapper, sir.'

'Correct,' said her uncle, breaking into a grin.

'Well, I'm happy to say I was right. Well flown, you monkey.'

'Thank you, sir. Oh, and sir, you were right about the lectures, too. We couldn't have escaped if Zawn hadn't gone to them. I won't bunk off any more.'

'Congratulations to you too, young Zawn. There'll be a commendation for both of you when you return to the Academy.' His face faded.

Trel and Zawn clasped hands in triumph. The ambassador looked at them quizzically.

'I suppose this was a kidnap and not an elopement?'

'You couldn't be more wrong, sir,' said Zawn earnestly.

'No,' said Trel. 'You haven't lost a daughter, but you have gained a son.'

'What is she talking about?' asked the ambassador.

'It's a long story,' said Zawn, 'but there'll be plenty of time to tell it on the way to Minerva. Hadn't we better get going?'

'Yes, Dad,' said Trel, 'and while he's telling you, do you think I could fly the ship?'

THE DEVIL OF WARG
by Elana Bregin

The creature stood black and furious in its steel cage. Its curved claws gripped the bars, its shackled hands straining uselessly to force them apart. Its bellowings had quietened now, but its drugged red eyes glared with sullen rage at the small crowd of men.

Robbie stood with the other Catchers, pouring spicy fruit-ale down his thirsty throat, ashamed to see how his arm still trembled from the effort of the capture.

'Go on, go on you black swine, struggle all you want. You'll not get those bars to bend for you, I guarantee it,' Big George grinned, as he helped himself to a second glassful of ale.

The devil-beast grinned back at him, showing its gleaming fangs.

'Look at them vampire's teeth of his! I'd like to knock them down his devil's throat, I would,' Sydon muttered, dabbing at his injuries with a dirty cloth.

'It's those mad paws I'm nervous of,' said Timmon with a shudder. 'Did you see what he did to Alec's arm?'

'Aye – pulled it clean out of its socket!' Big George growled. 'Gave one huge wrench and out it came. I've never heard such screaming!'

'He put up a good fight all right, damn him,' said Robbie's father, grudging admiration in his tone. 'A double-dose of dart-drug in him, outnumbered eight to one, and he still gave us a run for our money.'

'But we got you in the end, didn't we, Devil,' Sydon sneered. He picked up the long steel prodder and poked it viciously through the bars. The creature flinched tiredly at the blow. The sound of its hissing filled the tented room like snakes.

'Sydon – stop that! Leave the beast!' said Robbie's father sharply. 'I'll not have you baiting the Catches – I've told you before. There's no profit to be made from damaged stock – you should know that by now.'

'Just making sure it knows we're the masters here, that's all,' said Sydon sulkily. 'So it don't try no more of its sly tricks on us.'

He hadn't been half so brave out in the desert, Robbie remembered. When the creature first came bursting out of the sandcave in its terrifying charge, he'd been the first to lose his nerve.

'The Devil – it's the Devil – Oh Lord, save us – it's the Devil himself!' he'd screamed, trying to run and cross himself at the same time.

The resemblance was uncanny, though. Even Robbie's father had been unnerved, shooting the sedative dart way off its mark; as transfixed by the sight of the creature as everyone else. Its gleaming black body stood upright and tall, the fur seal-sleek, the chest and forearms muscled like a man's. Its face was ape-like, with a leathery skin patterned with snake-skin markings of green and black. A pair of short horns curved from its head. And its tail was long and thin, with a triangular barb on the end. It was the kind of prize that Catcher teams dreamed of. The AARD Centres – Alien Animal Research and Display – would pay good money indeed for such a crowd-drawing specimen.

Robbie felt none of the usual pity as he stared towards the captive. Just looking at it brought a superstitious shudder to his spine. There was something about this creature that invited cruelty, that made you *want* to jab at it and torment it and rejoice in its helpless rage.

'It's because we're afraid of it,' he thought. 'It's fear that makes us cruel.'

'Let's drink up, lads, and get to the ship,' Robbie's father said to his men. 'There's a load of work to be done if we're to be ready to leave by tomorrow's light. Robbie—' he said in softer tones, 'stay here, will you? Keep an eye out tonight. See no-one goes near that cage – I mean no-one. I'll not have a valuable specimen ruined by stupidity.'

His eyes, as he said it, were on Sydon, who stood still with the prodder in his hand, sending surly looks towards the Devil from his bloodshot eyes.

'Yes, sir,' Robbie said obediently. But his heart sank low at the prospect of staying there alone.

The men filed out. Robbie seated himself on a pile of food sacks and listened glumly to their voices dwindling into the distance. Soon he couldn't hear them any more, and there was only the wind's wail and the roaring of Warg's great ocean, beating itself against the marble-toothed cliffs. The captives watched him fearfully from their cages. The sand-creepers had stopped their unnerving sobbing now. The little blue-faced simians huddled fearfully, whimpering in each other's arms. The seacats squirmed in their pails of salty water. The rainbow birds sat shocked and still.

Robbie turned his eyes away from them uneasily, sternly fighting down his pity. This was the part of Catchers' work that worried him the most. The chase was always thrilling, the capture very satisfying. But he hated what came after: the sight of terrified creatures cringing wild-eyed in their cages, their crying and struggling to get free – knowing they would never be free again, that they would spend the rest of their days in exile from their home worlds, on display in AARD Centre cages. This sentimental streak in himself bothered Robbie a lot. It wasn't good in a Catcher. A good Catcher couldn't afford to let himself get soppy over his catches or he'd never catch anything at all. Robbie's father had told him that often enough.

A tired shiver of chains drew his eyes towards the Devil. It was seated now, squatting apelike on its haunches, its massive shoulders hunched, its brooding red stare fixed on him. Something about that stare brought shivers of uneasiness to Robbie's spine. It was so . . . alien. He imagined sly thoughts plotting evil plots, had to fight to remind himself that it was only an animal, not the sinister demon that it resembled. He got up off the sacks and walked slowly towards the creature.

'I'm not afraid of you,' he whispered. He said it louder. 'I'm not afraid of you, Devil,' he scowled.

It mocked him, mimicking his frown. It opened and closed its black mouth, copying his mouth movements vacantly, like an ape might, without understanding. He felt a sudden intense urge to pick up the prodder and ram it at the big black body, the way Sydon had; to watch the beast howl and writhe – and know that it was at his mercy.

He turned away and went to light the oil lamp – for the tent was full of evening gloom now. Timmon came by, bringing supper – a plateful of bird-stew and tubers, overcooked and tasteless. But Robbie wolfed it down, too ravenous to care. As he reached for the water canteen to slake his thirst, he heard the Devil hiss. It occurred to him that it might be thirsty. The drug always made them thirsty, and it had had nothing to drink since its capture. But he hardened his heart against the thought, muttering; 'Let it thirst. It will do it no harm to thirst, the Devil.'

Turning his back deliberately, he walked outside.

Warg's lilac dusk was deepening over the desert, sinking cold and quiet over the yellow dunes. The sunken sea tossed and heaved like a great green serpent against its cage of black marble. A cold salt wind swirled around Robbie's shoulders, lifting his black hair, making his hide jacket flap like caught wings. He lifted his head to look at the sky. The great red star Pirrhus V was rising in the east. Immediately overhead, he could see Warg's sister planets, Zephon and Xanthus, where the Catcher team had done their trapping before coming to Zarg. And somewhere beyond them, lost among the blazing thickets of stars, was the beautiful blue planet Earth – his father's homeworld, which Robbie himself had never seen. His whole life had been spent as a galaxy gypsy, wandering between strange planets and the huge floating space research colonies with his Catcher father. Craning his head back further, Robbie let his eyes scan through the glittering spread of stars: millions, billions of them in this one galaxy alone! And beyond this galaxy, countless other galaxies, each one with its own star billions, its satellite planets and moons and unexplored worlds. The idea of such immensity made Robbie feel giddy and strange. 'Perhaps,' he thought, 'on one of those worlds right now, an alien team of Catchers is busy trapping humans; cooking them for their food and skinning them for their clothes and putting them on display for some strange alien gathering to gawk at.' The thought gave him shivers of gooseflesh.

He went back into the tent. The little simians peeped at him with big eyes, whimpering as he passed. In the smoky light of the oil lamp, a frightening shadow loomed, cast huge and horned on the tent's canvas wall. Robbie whirled around. But it was only shadow. The Devil sat as he'd left it, safely chained to its cage. He turned his back on it and moved about the tent uneasily, rearranging sacks to make his bed. And all the while, he could feel the creature watching him, its hot stare fastened like a sly red dart between his shoulder-blades.

He lay down to sleep, leaving the oil-lamp burning. But sleep did not come easily. The captives were restless in their cages, whimpering and scuffling. The wind blew harder and the tent flapped and strained like a devil-creature trying to break free. Robbie lay tensely, listening to the sounds. Each time a chain clanked, he would shoot up nervously. Every sputtering of the oil lamp sounded to him like a demon's gloating hiss.

When he finally did drop off, his sleep was full of troubled dreams. The Devil was in all of them, with his vampire's grin and cruel clawed hands and sly red eyes. Sometimes, Robbie was his keeper. And sometimes, he was free and Robbie was running – endlessly running across unending miles of sand. But whether he was the pursuer or the prey was never clear.

Sounds woke him: frightened cries from the animals, a commotion of mumbling, cursing, thudding, stumbling. He sat up in fright. A figure loomed darkly in front of him. For one heart-jolting moment, he imagined it had the Devil's shape. Then he saw that it was human.

'Tha's right, tha's right – s'me, you evil beast,' a hoarse voice muttered. 'You remember me, don't you? Sydon – yer old pal Sydon.'

He stood liquor-soaked and swaying in front of the Devil's cage, his matted hair on end, the stink of him filling the tent.

Robbie got up and went towards him. 'Sydon,' he said. 'What are you doing here? Go back to the ship. Come, let me take you.'

He tried to grasp the man's arm. But he was shaken off like a fly. Sydon seemed hardly aware of him, all his drunken focus fixed on the caged creature before him.

'Get on yer feet when I speak to you, Devil! I said – on yer feet when yer master speaks, yer ignorant slime!'

He picked up the prodder and tried unsteadily to manoever it through the bars. But he was too drunk to aim it straight.

The Devil rumbled like uneasy thunder.

'Shut up!' Sydon shouted. 'I'll have no more of your mockery – you hear me, Beast? Oh – grin at me will yer! I'll teach you to grin! I'll make you swallow those vampire's teeth of yours, I will! I've put up with your tricks and torments all I'm going to. Now it's your turn.'

In his drunken state, he seemed to believe it was the real Devil he was talking to. His eyes were as wild as a madman's. He clanged the prodder viciously against the cage bars, trying again to insert it, and again failing.

'Sydon – enough! Come on now,' Robbie said worriedly, trying a second time to take his arm. But an unexpected blow sent him reeling backwards.

'Leave me – get out of my way!' Sydon roared in fury. He swung about him wildly with the prodder, almost knocking himself off balance, only just managing not to fall. 'I'll not be stopped – you hear me?' he muttered thickly. 'I'll show that mocking beast who's the master now. I'll send him back to the hell he came from – tha's what I'll do!' He threw down the prodder and snatched up something else.

'Dance, Devil,' he said thickly. 'Let's see you dance now. I've danced to your tune often enough. Now you can dance to mine.'

He heaved the thing he held between the cage bars. There was a sound of shattering, a heavy smell of lamp fuel. Animals screamed in terror as pitch darkness filled the tent. Sydon's spiteful chuckling echoed eerily. A match-head scraped.

'Sydon – no – what are you doing? *Don't!*' Robbie cried.

He made a desperate lunge. But he was too late. There was a dull sound of igniting. Flame flared through the Devil's cage, engulfing the creature in shivers of hungry fire. The Devil roared terribly, straining helplessly against its chains, beating its burning feet against the cage floor.

Sydon laughed, slapping his knees and staggering in drunken glee.

Robbie snatched up the prodder and felled him with a furious blow. He ran to the Devil's cage despairingly, raced away again to scrabble through dark corners for the cage keys, his torch. There was no time for thought or caution. With a trembling hand he unlocked the cage door, tore off his jacket and used it to beat down the small, hot pyre of flames. They died reluctantly, giving off black, acrid clouds of smoke. Eyes streaming, Robbie turned to look at the Devil. It lay slumped beside him on the cage floor, all twisted up in its chains, its head arched back against the bars, a deathly grimace on its face. The smell of its singed fur was sickening and strong. Robbie thought for one despairing moment that it was already dead. Then he heard its desperate gasping for breath – saw the reason for it. A section of chain was caught round its throat in a tight, choking noose. Its shackled hands made it impossible for the creature to free itself. If Robbie didn't do something – and quickly – it would strangle to death.

He crouched down cautiously beside it, playing his torchbeam over the strange, snake-patterned face; there was no reaction. His heart was beating with painful force. His skin crawled with revulsion to be so close to that dangerous, devil-horned head, but the helplessness of the big, injured body stirred his pity. The creature seemed barely conscious, barely alive. He could see the painful blisters on its legs and feet, its soles all bloody from trampling the shards of lantern glass. The wheezing of its breath sounded like a death rattle. Quickly Robbie found the key for the wrist manacles. He clicked the cuffs open, freeing the big, clawed hands; reached out nervously to pull the throttling chain from the creature's neck. Then he drew his hand back. Something about the creature's stillness did not seem right to him. He shone his torch suspiciously towards its face again; caught too late the gleam of cunning in the slitted eyes.

There was a violent eruption of movement beneath him. A shove of massive force thrust him backwards, slamming him up against the cage bars. For long seconds, he was too winded to move. The Devil's fearsome face loomed close to his. And he thought for a terrible moment that he was about to be devoured. Then, hissing, it drew back, threw off the loosened chains from its neck, and hobbled swiftly from the cage. By the time Robbie had found his breath again and staggered to his feet, the prisoner was gone.

Robbie raced frantically in pursuit. But the darkness outside the tent was empty. He shone his torch in all directions, hoping to pick up a shadow of fleeing movement. But he saw nothing. The night was full of roaring from the angry sea. The wild wind howled at him like a voice of fury. He felt like howling too. He couldn't believe how stupid he'd been – how *stupid*, to let himself be tricked so easily! He should never have opened the Devil's cage – no matter what the reason! He should rather have left it to burn and choke while he ran to call his father. But as usual, he had allowed his soft side to cloud his judgement. The thought of his father, what he would say when he discovered his prize exhibit gone, made Robbie quake with apprehension.

He bent to shine his torch at the ground. A trail of bloody footprints sped, huge and clawed, across the dark sand. But even as he stared at them, they were being erased, covered up by wind-blown sand. By the time he'd made it to the ship to raise the alarm, the trail would be dead. There'd be nothing to show which way the Devil had gone, no hope of tracking it. Robbie hurried into the tent despairingly. Sydon was lying where he'd left him, stretched like a corpse on the floor, half on his face. Robbie fell upon him urgently.

'Sydon – wake up – you must wake up!' he said. 'The Devil's gone – the Devil's escaped, Sydon. We have to go after it – Sydon, wake up! Wake up!'

Loud snores answered him. It didn't matter how he shouted and shook and pummelled, nothing could rouse the man from his drunken stupor. Robbie stayed kneeling beside him, looking down at him in frustration. Then he leapt up, searched around him for the dart-gun; snatched it up, and plunged outside.

There was no time to think about what he was doing. He was too angry for caution anyway. The one thought in his mind was that the Devil should not escape, should not be allowed to get away with its treachery. He had some vague plan of trying to track it to its lair, pumping it full of sedative, then running back to alert the others and lead them to it.

The stars sped with him as he ran. Distant volcanos spewed their fiery traces of lava against the dark horizon. But he had no eyes for their eerie beauty, all his concentration fixed on the footprints before him. He ran awkwardly, hunched over low to see the ground, the heavy dart-gun bumping painfully against his side. The sand dragged at his legs and the wind shoved him backwards with unfriendly force. Before long, he was exhausted. But the creature that he followed show no signs of faltering. Even in his anger, he felt a grudging admiration for its endurance, that it could run so swiftly and determinedly on its burnt and bloody feet. He sensed that he was lagging further and further behind it. The wind-blurred footprints were growing less and less distinct. Half the time, he wasn't even sure that they were footprints he was following, not just random dents in the sand. The black of the desert stretched like an unending abyss around him. He began to feel that he was in his dream, running and running for a reason he'd forgotten; chasing or being chased, he was no longer sure.

Once, when he turned to look behind him, he thought he saw eyes burning red and sly between the dunes. His heart leapt in shuddering fear. But when he shone his torch, there was nothing to see. Still the fear stayed with him. He kept imagining he heard the Devil's voice, whispering his name. Now, he ran because he dared not stop.

Slowly the black sand turned to purple beneath him. The wind died to a whisper. White streams of mist wreathed from the desert floor like ghostly birds. Robbie looked up dazedly, to see that Warg's dawn had come. The sky was full of deep pink and green. Morning stars burned fiercely above the desert shadows.

Robbie switched off his torch and stood shivering exhaustedly, straining his eyes through the gloom to try and get his bearings. There were no familiar landmarks here. The sea's voice roared distantly somewhere out of sight. Sandcliffs reared up coldly around him, their dim sides pitted with the yawning mouths of caves. The Devil could have gone to ground in any one of them. There was no sign of its footprints here; no hope of finding it now, Robbie knew that. And yet . . .

As he stood there in the hush of the desert morning, an uncanny feeling began to creep over him. The skin all over his body was suddenly crawling with gooseflesh. He felt the Devil's hidden stare on him. It was watching him – it was somewhere close – he could *feel* it!

Gripping the dart-gun tightly, he slowly spun around. Black rocks crouched behind him. From a nearby dunetop, a tremor of movement caught his eye. But it was only a scampering troop of simians. A pair of rainbow birds leapt suddenly into the sky, their shrill cries startling him so that he almost dropped the gun. Nervously, he backed towards the rocks, his whole body vibrating with that strange and eerie sense of danger.

A sound; so soft, he almost didn't hear it. He half-turned uneasily. Out of the corner of his eye, he saw one of the black rocks behind him rear up to take on the Devil's shape. A massive fist swung out

of the pink sky and knocked his head from his body. Blackness filled his sight.

He came to consciousness again very slowly, full of dread – afraid to open his eyes without knowing why. His head throbbed painfully and his ears seemed to be full of roaring and hissing. He was lying against stone, half propped up. He tried to move to a more comfortable position, but found he couldn't. His hands and legs were tightly bound with some strange, slippery substance. It felt like seaweed, but when he strained against it, it didn't give or break. An unbearable thirst burned in his mouth.

'Water—' he croaked hoarsely. 'Water.'

A sharp, familiar hissing answered him. He opened his eyes in terror. The Devil loomed in front of him, its fanged mouth grinning evily into his face. Behind it . . . were other Devils – dozens of them! All crowding round him, horned and terrible in the shadowy cavern light. Their hot red eyes blazed into his like lasers. The sound of their cruel hissing froze his blood. With terrible certainty, Robbie knew that he had to be in hell.

'Don't hurt me – please!' he whimpered to the Devils. But they mocked him, opening and closing their mouths in mimicry of his speech, rumbling at him with a sound like terrible laughter.

★　　★　　★

Oorahr, chieftain of the Wargoon desert tribe, stood frowning in the blue gloom of the cavern entrance, watching the creature – alone now, and thinking itself unregarded – as it struggled exhaustedly against its sea-twine bonds.

'I thought you said these aliens were intelligent,' he growled softly to Auroo, who stood beside him, restlessly shifting on his sore and blistered feet.

'They are,' Auroo grunted back. 'Only intelligent creatures could exchange talk the way they do, could be so cunning . . . and so cruel.'

'Yet this one seems very stupid to me,' Oorahr rumbled.

'It shows no sign of understanding anything we say to it. Even when we make its own speech-faces back to it, it only grows more frantic. Why can it not realize we mean it no harm?'

'Fear makes it stupid,' Auroo said. 'It thinks we intend to enslave it – or devour it – as its own kind does with others.'

'I worry,' said Oorahr, deepening his frown. 'I do not trust the treacherous nature of this thing. What if it should break free? Lead its whole ferocious tribe back here to annihilate or enslave us all? Perhaps we should kill it now, Auroo, while we have the chance?'

'No!' said Auroo. His red stare brooded silently on the captive. 'No!' he slowly said again. 'It does not deserve death.'

He saw Oorahr's look of surprise. 'You can say

that? After all you suffered at the hands of these creatures?'

Auroo was silent for a moment. 'I owe my freedom to this creature,' he said gruffly. 'It showed me pity when others of its kind would not have done. When I was burning in the fire, it ran to save me. It was afraid of me – yet still it risked itself to save my life.' He shook his black, horned head in bafflement. 'What kind of beings are these, Oorahr, that can be so cruel, and yet . . . compassionate too?'

'If we could find some way past this one's great mistrust of us, we might find out,' said Oorahr, shrugging.

Auroo nodded. 'I would like to know its thoughts,' he said softly. 'I would like to understand the world such creatures come from. It may be that we have things to teach each other.'

Picking up a water-gourd from a stone shelf, he hobbled slowly towards the captive. 'Do you thirst, little alien?' he rumbled in his most soothing cadences. 'No, don't shrink away from me. I intend no hurt to you.'

He saw fear twisting in the creature's strange, pale face, leaping like a wild, trapped beast in the white-rimmed circles of its eyes. Gently he lifted the gourd up to the parched and panting mouth, and gave it drink.

KARLA

by Allan Frewin Jones

'Rolek!' Karla ran, her heart pounding, feet hammering on the metal skyway. It was her brother. The Fibians were taking her brother Rolek. He was being held limply between two Fibian soldiers, his head hanging, his feet dragging as they marched him to a hovering kopta. The soldiers' grotesque faces lifted as they heard her cry and one of them brandished a long-clawed fist at her. The hideous green frog-eyes swivelled to pinpoint her – but still she ran towards them. She couldn't let them take him. Not after all this time of hiding and planning for the fight back.

The wide, lipless mouths of the Fibian soldiers gaped. She knew what would come next, but she didn't pause. It was over in a second. The tongues, four metres long, lashed out, striking her chest and forehead – sending her crashing backwards. Semi-conscious, skidding helplessly on the smooth skyway. She came jarringly to a halt only inches from the lip of the metal track. For a second her swimming eyes saw the ground a dizzying one hundred metres down before she lost consciousness.

Time passed. Karla groaned and lifted herself. She must have been unconscious for hours. The twin suns of Melloon had set and the six huge moons hung shimmering in the dark yellow sky. The kopta was gone. She stood up, swaying, still feeling the ache of the blows from those two alien tongues. The door of their cabin hung open, twisted on one broken hinge.

She had lost him. She walked unsteadily into their living area. The place was in chaos. Their sparse furniture overturned – the damp reek of the Fibians hanging thickly in the air and the slime from their long, deadly tongues dripping from the walls. Rolek must have put up a fierce fight. Karla slumped against the wall, the stench turning her stomach. This was no place to be any more.

'Listen, Karla.' She could almost hear Rolek's strong, calm voice. 'It's only a matter of time before they get me. You've got to get away. Get right away from the city. Up into the hills. Find a refugee camp. You'll be safe there. The city is too dangerous for a kid.'

'I'm not a kid,' Karla would say, glaring at him.

'I'm ten years old. You're only six years older than me and you mean to fight them. I'm not leaving you.' And she would grin. 'Besides – someone's got to look after you.'

The Fibians had come out of nowhere. Out of the dark yellow of the night sky. With no warning. The great whiteish globe hanging like a foul-smelling bubble above the soaring steel buildings of the city. The Fibian invaders oozing out of the flabby underbelly of the spoorship in their slime-stained koptas. They carried no weapons. They stood taller than human height with their long crooked, gangling arms and legs and their soft, green, swollen bellies. Their broad, wide-mouthed heads squatted on their narrow shoulders. Bulbous eyes gleamed with alien intelligence. They didn't need to carry weapons. They had those long, powerful tongues which could coil chokingly around a human neck or lash out as hard as clubs.

In the months that followed, the people of Melloon learned more about the invaders. A gigantic mothership roosted unseen, high in the sky over every continent. It was from these colossal monsters that the horrible spoorships descended. The koptas came and went through a sucking, mouth-like valve at the base of the spoorships. Apart from that single entrance, the spoorships were featureless.

A spoorship hung over every city. The people of Melloon were defenceless against them. This was a colony that had abandoned warfare when they had left Earth five hundred years ago. A planet of sparkling, peaceful cities – of darting silver skyboats and great expanses of calm blue ocean. Why would the people of Melloon need weapons? How could they know that one terrible night the sky would be filled with invaders from another world?

Thousands had died on that first night. The Fibians were merciless. They took no prisoners. They cared nothing for human life. The five-hundred-year-old Earth colony was overwhelmed within a month. Those that could had fled to the hills – hoping against hope that they would not be pursued. Those few that remained in the cities went into hiding, doing their best to sabotage the invaders, to slow down the inexorable conquest.

Karla's father had gone out one night to join up with a group of saboteurs. Her mother had wanted to go with him, to fight beside him. The last thing Karla remembered her father saying was, 'No!' Holding her mother by her shoulders. 'No. I'm expendable. You aren't. You *know* things.' He had never come back.

Her mother had worked at the secret rocket base before the Fibians had come. As far as Karla's family had known, her mother was the last of the Guardians to have survived the invasion. Only she knew the code that would bring the rockets up out of their underground silos.

When the rockets were at rest on their hidden launch-pads they were invisible to all but those few Guardians who knew the secret.

Constructed when the colony had been in its infancy, the rockets had been the fail-safe escape method, dug deep in the outskirts of the first city, their existence unknown to any but a select few. The rocket base had been built because no-one had known in those early days whether Melloon would prove a safe planet to colonize: constructed in secret because the leaders at the time had not wanted potential colonizers to guess that there were any doubts about the safety of this paradise planet.

The rockets had stood unused through the centuries as the colony expanded to cover the planet. Grassed-over and used as a recreation area, very few people knew that, beneath their feet, the age-old escape rockets were kept primed for an emergency.

The rocket command centre, disguised as just another civil service office, had been destroyed early on in the invasion. Only Karla's mother had survived the devastation.

Their hope had been to gather all those in the city who had lived through the invasion; gather them together and use the rockets to escape the Fibians.

Disease had swept the city in the wake of the invasion. No amount of hiding had saved their mother. The Fibians hadn't killed her. She had died from drinking bad water. But not before she had managed to whisper the Code to her children. The Code that would open the silos and free the rockets.

And so Rolek had taken on the task of trying to bring the survivors together. And with her mother and father dead, Karla had stayed with him. She saw no point in trying to escape into the hills. Why run and hide? Once the Fibians had cleared the cities of human life, they would turn those dreadful, bulging eyes on to the hills. Why put death off by hiding? That's what Karla thought, and that was why she had stayed with her brother.

And now he was gone. Karla lifted her head, a defiant light in her eyes. They had not killed him. They had taken him away. It could only mean one thing. They intended to question him. To get information out of him about the other rebel bands in the city. He was probably there now, in the dank white spoorship. They were probably doing dreadful things to him – torturing him for names and places – for the details that would enable them to clear the city once and for all.

'No,' said Karla to herself. 'I won't let that happen. I *won't*.'

She gathered together all the food she could carry and that the Fibian slime hadn't contaminated. Filling her backpack she left their wrecked cabin, determined somehow to find Rolek and to rescue him.

She looked cautiously around. None of the koptas were visible above the high towers. The spoorship

110

had come to ground in the open recreation area beneath which the secret rocket base lay hidden, bouncing slightly and quivering as if it was made out of something soft and disgusting. When grounded the spoorship would lift itself on a tripod of flabby, mushroom-white stalks to allow the koptas to get out – and to allow the few prisoners they captured to be taken inside. No prisoner had ever come out again.

Once, some months ago, a group of brave rebels had attacked the grounded ship. But the fleshy outer surface had proved impenetrable from outside. Koptas full of Fibians had emerged, bursting out of the valve-mouth that closed itself behind them. Not one of that rebel group had survived.

In the long yellow Melloonian nights, crouched in their lonely cabin, Rolek and Karla had often discussed ways of attacking the spoorship. Its similarity to a bubble had given Karla an idea. 'Couldn't something be fired into it?' she had said. 'Something sharp – maybe it would burst?'

Rolek had laughed and had irritatingly ruffled her cropped brown hair. 'Don't be silly,' he had said. 'There isn't anything in the city powerful enough to do that.' But the idea had stuck in Karla's brain. After all – hadn't a few Fibian soldiers been killed in a similar way by people running at them with sharpened steel spikes? Driving them into the bloated bellies and cheering as the creatures burst apart and fell dead. If a sharpened pole could kill a Fibian, then why couldn't a bigger version of the same thing destroy one of their spoorships?

That was the thought that ran through Karla's mind as she crept out into the dangerous night in search of her captured brother.

She had a plan. She might well die in the process – but then she knew she would die sooner or later anyway. So why not go down fighting?

The hidden rocket base was buried deep beneath the south side of the city. She had learned rocketry at school, earning the highest marks in her class as she sat in the instruction cabin and guided her computer-simulated rocket out of port and up into the sky. How different could it be to guide a *real* rocket? Not one of the commercial travel rockets that plied their trade back and forth from the spaceport. They had all been destroyed. Karla was thinking of those *other* rockets. The ones of which the Fibians were unaware.

She ran crouching along the skyway to the elevator tower. Drifting faintly over the silence of the city she could hear the honks and croaks as the Fibians communicated with one another – an eerie sound that made her flesh creep. The spoorships communicated in a similar way, sending their booming notes deafeningly through the sky until sometimes all you could do was throw your hands over your ears and scream for the noise to stop.

She swung herself out into the empty throat of the

tower and climbed down the long knotted rope that had been for months their only method of entrance and exit. Hand over hand she lowered herself to ground level and came out into the maze of deserted streets. The wreckage of the one-sided war was everywhere. Streetboats overturned. Mangled hunks of metal. Splinters of glass. Rubbish strewn about. The dark long-dried stains of conflict. In the distance she saw a squad of Fibians strutting across a side street. Their ungainly, bobbing walk filled her with revulsion. It would look funny if it weren't so deadly. They didn't look as if they should be upright – they looked like creatures that ought to be crawling about on all fours.

She flattened herself in a doorway. She could hear their raucous croaks and see the neck-membranes inflating and deflating as they spoke to each other. They were so close she could even hear the wet sucking of their great splayed feet on the ground.

She waited until they were out of sight then made a run for it. It would take her several hours to get over to the rocket base. She would have to hide during daylight hours. The twin suns bleached everything to a searing whiteness and the koptas would be floating across the sky searching for rebels.

She carried on moving until the last of the six moons fell out of sight and then she hunted for a secure place to secrete herself.

It was a supermarket. Its windows smashed and its

doors broken in, the shelves had long ago been cleared of anything edible and what was left was scattered about and trampled. She went through to an old stockroom and then, amongst the boxes, she settled herself to try and sleep the day away.

She was awoken occasionally by the echoing boom of the faraway spoorship sending orders to the koptas, and once by the sound of a squad of Fibians passing the shopfront. But no-one came into her dark back room. She had bad dreams – but then bad dreams were normal these days. The worst dreams were of life before the invasion: swimming in the deep blue ocean on whose shores the city had been built; laughing and swimming with Rolek and with their mother and father and their friends. Where were all her friends? She didn't think one of them had survived. Not unless they were alive somewhere up in the hills. She woke from these dreams with tears running down her face.

In the soft yellow moonlit glow of another night Karla crept from her hideaway and set off for the final run to the rocket base. The uncanny howls and grunts of the Fibian hunting squads sounded all around her. They were out in force tonight. Crouched trembling behind a crashed streetboat, she watched in horror as a man ran from house to house at the far end of the street, pursued by the lumbering soldiers. A tongue flickered out, slithery and lithe as a worm in the moonlight. It coiled around the man's neck and he

114

was pitched over backwards. Karla looked away. At least it meant they were too busy to spot her as she darted off into deeper cover. The thought filled her with guilt. Another man dead – and her running as fast and as far as she could in the opposite direction.

She reached the deserted stretch of parkland in the middle of the long Melloonian night. A few months ago the daylight hours would have seen this place teeming with people. Even the nights would have been lit up with bonfires and fireworks. But now it was desolate as only an abandoned playground can be.

On the far side of the open ground Karla could see the spoorship, seeming to wobble on its squat legs. A big, flattened beachball a thousand metres across and filled with horrors.

Much nearer, the ruined shell of the building where her mother had worked held up ragged fangs to the night, moonlight gleaming through the empty windows.

Karla picked her way through the rubble. Her mother's dying words echoed in her head. Instructions given to her children on how to get down into the real heart of the building. Rocket control. Chunks of masonry blocked her way, but Karla was determined not to be thwarted this close to her goal.

She spent two exhausting hours scrabbling through the wreckage. At last, sweating and filthy, she found the stairway – the stairway down which they had

intended to lead the ragged survivors. But now Karla
had other plans. There was nothing to lose. If Rolek
was forced to reveal their plans for escape, all would
be lost anyway. The others – whatever *others* there
might be – would have to wait. Karla's only thought
was of the rescue of her brother.

The underground silo had its own power source,
powered by massive generators sunk deep in concrete. Karla ran her hand over a light sensor and a
blessed glow lit the stairway. The generators had
survived.

She stumbled down to the steel door and tapped
out her mother's private code. The door hissed
smoothly open. A series of brightly lit rooms was
revealed. Rooms she had never seen. Rooms that
no-one alive in the city even knew existed, banked
with computer terminals and rank after rank of
towering, silent electronic equipment.

She ran through the control complex, searching
for the master-console.

A huge black window stretched in front of her.
She licked her lips and wiped her sweating hands on
her hips, her eyes roving over the control panel.
Think. Think. What had her mother told them?

She traced her fingers over the panel of coloured
dials. The black window burst into light and she
stared out at an unbelievable sight.

Out on the vast underground launchfield the
rockets stood on their tails, their shining arrow-sharp

shapes tinted yellow by the floodlights, their shadows forming a complex maze of light and dark.

She pressed out the Code and entered it. In the silence that followed she had time to wonder whether she had misremembered her mother's instructions. But then she saw it.

Dark crescents were opening in the roof – opening into black holes. A thousand black pits in the lofty metal roof.

She ran to the door that led to the launchfield, as the light from the silo poured upwards into the night sky.

She came to the first of the towering rockets. She knew how to enter the rocket and how to climb hand over hand up to the gyroscopic control booth. She grinned, worn out but thrilled to have got this far. It was all exactly as she remembered it from school. Her hands flicked over the console. Red, green and yellow lights ignited on the panels that surrounded her and a low hum sounded from beneath her. She felt the rocket tremble around her. Biting her lip, she eased down on the joystick. Just like at school – except that this was for real.

She glanced from the porthole. The launchfield looked like a cavern filled with stalagmites as her rocket gently eased itself into the air, as smooth as a fish through water.

As she eased the rocket up through its escape port and into the dark sky, she heard a sudden bellow from the nearby spoorship. The lights from the underground silo breached the night like searchlights fanning up into the sky.

Keep calm, Karla, she whispered to herself. You're almost there. She eased the throttle and the rocket leaped high. Through the porthole she saw the launchfield lights dwindle into a pincushion of sparks that could have fitted into her hand. The city wheeled. The air was full of the alarmed croaking roar of the spoorship, now no bigger than a golfball beneath her.

She had to disable the spoorship while it was on the ground. If Rolek was on board and her plan worked with the spoorship in the air, the destruction of the ship would doom him as well. She had to be quick.

She twirled the joystick fiercely forwards and the whole world, city, moons and all, spun around her as the rocket cut a tight curve through the night and pointed itself earthwards.

'This is it!' she shouted. 'I'm coming to *get* you!' The rocket hurtled towards the slowly rocking spoorship. 'Rolek!' she yelled. 'It's me! I'm coming to rescue you!' Adrenalin rushed through her – swamping her fear. 'I can do it,' she hissed between gritted teeth. 'I can *do* it!'

There was only the one chance. Another few seconds and the spoorship would be rising into the air. The clamour of the alerted spoorship filled her ears. Closer and closer, until the trembling white mass filled the viewscreen.

At the moment of impact she yanked back on the joystick. There was a huge, wet, splashing boom. The rocket shuddered and almost halted, flinging Karla from side to side as she fought to keep the joystick against her body. Slime and worse things splattered on the viewscreen and against the portholes and the deafening croaking changed to a screech that sounded like anger or pain.

She fought with the controls for a few desperate seconds before the rocket cleared the slime and sped again into the clear sky.

She wiped sweat out of her eyes. Fibian filth coated the portholes. She turned the rocket and slowed down, circling to discover the effects of her attack. The quivering hide of the spoorship was unbroken. Her attack had failed. The skin had proved too strong. But then she saw. The force of her impact had toppled the Spoorship off its tripod of stalk-like legs. It lay rolling slightly and misshapen, on its side, the legs dangling uselessly in the air.

Koptas were bursting out of the exit valve in panic, fountaining into the air, colliding and exploding. Some of them dived straight into the ground, popping with a soft sucking sound. Laughing and shouting, Karla circled the collapsing spoorship. She had done it. But how long would it be before the spoorship righted itself?

And Rolek was still inside!

The spoorship was screaming continuously now, sending out a distress signal that reverberated from city to city. Help would come and then all would be lost.

Karla slowed the rocket and engaged the landfall mechanism. She had got one hundred per cent for this manoeuvre at school – acting out on the computer the tricky business of tipping the rocket on to its tail and bringing it safely to earth. But could she do it in real life – amongst the scattering and exploding koptas and with the screech of the spoorship battering her ears?

She watched the landfall screen. The beam hit the ground square and the rocket slowly sank. It came to earth with a bump – not a bad landing in the cirumstances.

A lava-like spillage was gushing from the gaping mouth of the spoorship, spreading out over the ground like crawling glue. If she stepped into *that* she would be sucked under in an instant.

Her only chance lay in the rocket's tiny relief capsule. Shaped like a blunt-nosed torpedo, it had room enough for two people stretched out flat on their stomachs.

She edged herself inside. The capsule had two functions. One was for a simple escape from the rocket, and the other was to allow access to the outside for repairs. To enable the capsule to return to the rocket, a grapplebeam could be engaged. It would allow the capsule to move freely – but with the flick of a switch would reel the capsule back in to safety.

At least, she hoped that was what would happen.

She grasped the control stick and jabbed her thumbs down on the ignition disc.

The capsule catapulted from the side of the rocket. She spun the controls, weaving and diving as the koptas cartwheeled and crashed about her.

She aimed for the spluttering mouth of the spoorship. She felt the weight of the slime raining down on her, making it hard for her to keep control.

The inside of the spoorship was like the inside of a living body. Soft-walled chambers with valves opening wetly one into the other. Fibian bodies lay twitching and writhing – and still more Fibians crawled and leaped about in panic.

Her face hardened into a cold grin. Whatever happened now, she had taught them a lesson they wouldn't forget in a hurry.

Wrestling with the control stick she sent the capsule careering through quivering stomach-rooms and along intestinal corridors, searching desperately for Rolek.

The corridors and the slurping, dripping rooms seemed to go on for ever. If the grapplebeam failed, her chances of ever getting out of there alive were almost non-existent.

She was moving too swiftly for any of the stamped-ing Fibians to attack her — and those that did get in her way were sent tumbling through the thick air, broken and limp as rags.

And then she saw him. Scrambling along a tunnel wall, falling and picking himself up again like some-one trying to keep their feet on a shaken mattress. Rolek!

She yanked on the control stick and brought the capsule to a skidding halt.

She wrenched the lever that split the capsule open.

'Rolek! Here! Quickly!'

Two Fibians stopped in their headlong flight to escape the upended mayhem of the spoorship and loped towards them.

Rolek flung himself at the capsule and crashed in beside Karla.

As the capsule snapped shut, two sticky tongues slammed against the outside.

'Get us out of here!' gasped Rolek.

Karla slapped the grapplebeam button. The capsule throbbed, shaking them to their bones.

One of the Fibians threw itself at them. It came thudding down where the capsule had been lying only a second before.

Karla and Rolek clung helplessly on to one another as the capsule zigzagged and spun itself backwards through the heart of the spoorship.

There was no way of controlling it now the

grapplebeam was engaged. Karla hung on to Rolek – convinced that they would never get out.

Seconds seemed like hours as they sped through the guts of the stricken spoorship. There was no up or down any more – there was just horrible, endless chaos.

And then – miraculously – they were out into the clean night air.

There was a huge concussion as the capsule shot back into the rocket and came to a jarring halt.

Rolek was lying spreadeagled on the floor by the capsule, covered in slime and gasping for breath. She heaved him on to his back. 'Rolek! It's me!'

Rolek gasped. 'Karla? How?'

She grabbed his jacket and shook him. 'It's like I always said – you need me to look after you!' She hugged him, breathless with relieved laughter.

'Quickly now,' he said. 'Let's get out of here.'

'Did they hurt you?'

'A bit. They planned to start working on me tomorrow. They were waiting for their commander to get back. I was lucky.' He clambered up. 'Lucky to have a genius for a sister. How did you manage it?'

Karla grinned. 'Oh, it was easy.'

'We'd better head for cover. There's still enough of those koptas around to bring us down. I'll drive.'

'No you won't,' said Karla. 'This is *my* rocket.'

Rolek smiled. 'Always got to be in charge, eh? OK, captain – what's the plan?'

'Head for the hills,' said Karla. 'Now we know we can fight back we can convince people to raid the city, get more rockets – hidden rockets from other cities – launch a thousand of them all over the planet and attack every single one of those horrible bubble-things.'

She sat at the control panel, Rolek at her side, and steered the rocket up and away from the city, pointing its glittering nose towards the hills and the hope of her planet's survival.

'Look!' shouted Rolek.

Through the slime-stained viewscreen they saw one – two – no, three spoorships glistening like wet moons in the distance. Growing larger as they neared the speeding rocket.

'We're not out of trouble yet,' said Rolek.

Scores of koptas gouted from the approaching spoorships, gliding silently – adjusting their flight to swarm in pursuit of the escaping rocket.

Karla jammed both feet down on the booster panel and the two of them were thrust back in their seats as the rocket leaped forwards.

'Don't worry!' shouted Karla as they flashed like a knife-blade through the dark Melloonian night. 'I'll get us out of this.'

Rolek grinned at her. 'You're some kind of a girl, Karla,' he said.

'You bet I am!' said Karla as they pulled away from the speeding koptas and towards the distant sanctuary of the hills.

PERFECT HOST
by Nicholas Fisk

The following manuscript was passed to us by the widow of Corporal Ronald Arthur Meekins, RAOC, British Army. Cpl Meekins came by it in 1945 when the war against Hitler's Germany ended. He regarded it as a war souvenir, a mere curio.

The manuscript takes the form of a long roll of teleprinter paper, all in capitals. We have edited it to a more usual form, adding punctuation and translations where necessary.

. . . The best time of all was when I lived in a mallard duck. That was my revelation.

Ducks walk, swim and fly. Therefore they see and feel the best of everything Earth has to offer.

You earthlings, you humans – how can you be so

blind? How can you fail to see the wonders, the splendours, the glories, of your planet Earth? Why are you not dancing and singing – giving praise with your heads flung back to the radiant sky – all your waking hours?

Even a duck knows better than you.

This incredible world of yours – what do you do with it? I shall tell you. You scar and mutilate it. You tear holes in it. You hurt and kill beings that live on it – even other humans.

Mad.

You should see the world I came from! That would change your ideas! My world . . . you would not call it a world. A lump, a thing, a small ugly blob lost in the immensity of space. A raw, ugly little thing forever falling to pieces.

Not that I care if it crumbles to dust. We – I mean, the units like myself, the ones with some spark of hope and adventure left in us – we deserted our world long ago.

We formed into a Cluster.

We linked energies – cried 'GO!' – and spat ourselves into infinity, braving hunger, increasing feebleness and the countless random enemies that every traveller must meet in the empty wilderness.

How many of us in our Cluster? Fifteen thousand when we left. Today's count is 13,465. Tomorrow's?

Say, 13,100. And in not many years' time? Zero, did you say? No-one left?

Ah, no, my friend! Wrong! We will survive. Our numbers and powers will grow. At last we shall dominate your heaven-sent, beautiful planet. We will become its rulers.

Thanks to *me*.

You are curious about me? You would like to meet me?

Here I am. No, *here*.

You still can't see me? I am about the size and shape of a .177 airgun pellet. Easily missed!

To make things more difficult for you, I can change my shape. Now I am a thread, a filament; now, a tiny cube.

To make things quite impossible for you – I am hidden *inside* someone. Yes, you heard me correctly. Inside, hidden within a living body. My host.

Inside who, you ask? I will tell you later. When I tell, you will understand why I am so confident about the future of myself, the Cluster and my race.

About the Cluster. It is very simple. You know about ants and bees? You know they live collective lives, each belonging completely to their hives and colonies? All for one, one for all.

So you understand me. I am a unit of the Cluster. I could introduce you to a unit not far away who lived inside a boy who owned an airgun. That is how *I* know about .177 pellets and *he* knows about mallard ducks. The fool shoots at them.

How am I able to use this teleprinter – a machine designed for enormous human hands? Easy. Some units decided collectively to explore the machine's workings. The cables, the wires, they discovered, contained the messages. The keys are merely triggers. I am able to make a direct input of messages. I am doing it now. I need no keys, no 'triggers' – just the power of the Cluster.

Mind you, it was *I* and *I* alone who made the historic discovery. *I* was the one who entered the body of the human who is to be the saviour of his race – my race – perhaps the universe itself!

Quite certainly, when the future history of Earth comes to be written, my name will be writ large.

Back to the mallard duck.

No, come back with me even earlier. My first Earth host was a fish. The Cluster plunged from space into the sea. A fish, attracted by my wrigglings, swallowed me.

A second fish ate the first fish and me with it. Being in a fish is boring. Fishes think of nothing but eating, mating and surviving. So I let myself go blank: that is, I went into Recharge. You humans call it Sleep. But Recharge can last for months. Years, even.

When I 'awoke', the Cluster told me that nothing

of interest happened in the sea. The land was the place. I made my way ashore.

My first land-creature host was a mouse. It gobbled me up. I settled in its stomach then made my way to its head and brain. I remember how the mouse coughed and heaved during my journey. To a mouse, I must seem quite a big obstruction.

A cat named Tipples (because the tip of its tail was missing) ate the mouse and so became my host. Tipples was superb. It spent most of its life in cushioned slumber, and the rest demanding and getting food, attention and caresses.

One day Tipples, having nothing better to do, decided to over-eat until it was sick. It spewed me out and scratched earth over the discharge. I was left under a mound of wet soil by the edge of a lake.

Ducks lived on and by that lake. A mallard duck swallowed me.

Oh, the wonders it showed me!

Oh, the welcome of the waters into which we dived! – the rippling bliss when we paddled – the look, the taste, the smell, the feel of the lake!

And oh!, most wonderful of all, *flight*! Here I am, a mote in the duck's eye, soaring above blue water and green fields, zooming over red roofs and those magical silver ribbons called railway lines! Here I am again, perched in one of those little holes in the beak

(I fitted perfectly) learning the feel of speed, wind, high, low, onward and onward!

But then there had to be a human with a gun. My duck host was suddenly a body, definitely and pointlessly dead.

Now the Cluster said that mankind was the highest form of Earthlife – I must enter a human body. Still mourning the duck, I obeyed.

My first human host was a baby called Diddums, Darling, William, Superman or Boofuls. I did not discover which of these names was the correct one. It hardly mattered to me, as I soon realized that the baby amounted only to a *sketch* of mankind. To see the true picture, I needed an adult.

I passed myself, via a feeding bowl, from son to mother. She seemed filled with a strange human quality called Love. Often, this Love was inconvenient to her; she had to sacrifice herself and her wishes to others. We do not have Love on our planet, I am glad to say.

One way of showing Love is kissing. The mother often kissed the baby and its father. It was in this way – from her mouth to his – that I entered the male human, the father. I made my way to his brain.

It turned out that I was fortunate in my new host. He was an important, clever person, member of an Embassy. This meant that he travelled to foreign countries to discuss war, peace, trade, politics and other unnecessarily complicated human matters.

I accompanied him on one of these visits abroad – a fact of world-shaking significance.

Come with me, inside the father, to a splendid Embassy. Already I am dissatisfied with my host. Clever, intelligent, able and important though he is, he pales to nothing when in the company of someone much greater and stronger; a person listened to, respected and feared by the millions over whom he ruled, and by other nations he threatened with conquest.

This person, the host of my host in the Embassy, is the one for me! This is the human I must inhabit!

How? Adult humans, unlike human babies, are disciplined and restrained in their eating habits. Nevertheless, they may sometimes cough, choke or spill things.

It was a mild choking fit over a plate of salted almonds that allowed me to leave my ambassador host and enter the body of the powerful human who had so immediately impressed me. My first host coughed; my second host picked up and ate an almond on which I had been ejected from the mouth of the ambassador.

Thus I was carried into the greatest human in the history of the world.

★   ★   ★

My new host was a small male person with lank, dark hair and a small moustache. He looked insignificant; all the more so because he dressed so simply. All those around him were splendid with dress swords, gold froggings, medals and orders – even plumed hats. My man made no display of any sort.

Yet he was the central figure – the one person eyed by the beautiful ladies, and observed with anxious, sidelong glances by the important men.

Why was this small, pale, plainly dressed man the focus of attention?

Come with me to a great parade.

Here they come! The marching bands, blaring brass, throbbing drums, glittering symbols carried high above the robot-like marchers!

For whom do the bands play? For *him*, the Leader.

You see his warriors, rank upon rank, thousands upon thousands, marching as one . . .

For whom have they sworn to fight and die? The Leader.

'Machines!' you might say. 'The marching men are barely human!' You would be right. These humans are machines of world conquest, triggered by a single will.

Whose will? The Leader's.

Machine-men: and machine weapons. The machine weapons roll through the wide streets, growling, blattering, rumbling. Unstoppable, these machines! See how their treads tear and crush the very stones of that historic highway! See how their massive guns dip and bow in salute!

Whose machines? The Leader's.

The hours pass. Still the great parade goes by and the adoring crowds cheer themselves hoarse and raise their arms – every arm the same arm, each a rigid slanting weapon with a blade-like hand as its spear-head.

Raised to whom? The Leader.

A great silence falls, broken only by the flutterings of scarlet banners displaying the symbol of a crooked cross. The Leader is to speak . . .

Hear him! Thrill to that voice, echoing and re-echoing from the loudspeakers, flooding over the multitude! Hear what that harsh, indomitable voice promises!

An empire that will last a thousand years . . .

Yes! Yes!

One State, one people, one Leader . . . !

Yes! Yes!

The righting of old wrongs and humiliations . . . the annihilation of foul enemies, within and around us . . . the triumph of the Master Race . . . !

Yes, yes, yes! Hail, hail, hail the Leader!

And thousands of right arms and hands, like spears, are raised in identical salutes.

Even I, an alien being, could thrill to the Leader's words. Even I – a mere irritation in the corner of his eye, his piercing, all-seeing, blue orb – could understand the inevitable rightness of his message.

You say you cannot? I shall explain.

The Leader, alone among humankind, understood the Great Truth – the Truth we have always known among *my* race: 'The Cluster is all. I am nothing.'

You humans, you wise fools and spoiled babies, have chosen to ignore the Great Truth. Yet even ants and bees live by it. Humans – no: they think they know better. They regard themselves as *individuals*.

The conceit! The folly! The vanity!

Now listen to the Leader. *One State, one people, one Leader.* But of course! One and one only. Therefore, obey, obey, obey.

Listen again. *The triumph of the Master Race.* Repeat the words. Let their meaning flood your brain. You understand now? Yes, good – *of course* there can only be a single leader, a single Master Race for you to serve.

How else can you prevent humans acting pointlessly, ineffectively? How else get rid of the fallacy of the individual?

How else can you achieve the glorious aim of world domination, world sanity, world obedience to the Leader?

That is how the Leader thinks – how *we* think – how *I* think. Is there any other way of thinking?

★   ★   ★

Then, for me, tragedy.

The Cluster spoke. 'Leave your present home,' it told me.

Leave the Leader . . . !

For once I nearly committed the sin of arguing. 'Please,' I said, 'surely you must see the vital interest and importance of my present position?'

'We have another host for you,' the Cluster replied.

'But the future of the planet Earth rests on the shoulders of my host!'

'We have another host for you,' the Cluster replied. 'You are to enter the body of General So-and-so.'

I was stunned. I hardly heard – I still cannot remember – the name of my new host. 'When may I return to the body of the Leader?' I implored.

'When you are told to. If you are told. Now move.'

'But—'

'That is all.'

And that *was* all. During a meeting of the Leader and his military commanders, I entered the General's body and mind. The body was mouldering – the General drank – and the mind was crafty, stupid and 'individual'.

I was not surprised when, one night, the General's bedroom door was flung open – when men in long leather coats, carrying torches and hand-guns, word-lessly bundled my General into a car which took him to a dank and glistening cellar in a gloomy building – when they beat him almost to death, then shot him, then hung his dead body on a hook.

Even I could see how ridiculous the body looked, dangling there. And I could immediately understand why the Leader had ordered the General's destruc-tion. An example had to be made. The Leader would not tolerate slackness, treachery, 'individualism'.

And here was the example, hanging from a meat-hook.

When the men beat the General, he vomited. I flowed from him to the floor of the cellar. A rat ate me.

This was convenient. The rat lived in the sewers, the same sewers used by the palace of the Leader. So though the Cluster's new instructions did not men-tion the Leader, now that the General was dead I saw no reason not to do what I most wanted – to be once again inside the greatest being on the planet Earth. I can change shape. I can wiggle, swim, locomote . . .

I am close to him now, as I put these words into the teleprinter. I reside in the body of a woman whom the Leader favours. They are often together.

And what is, the news? The Leader is well into his crusade of world domination. His warriors, human and machine, advance from victory to victory.

Already the continent called Europe is almost entirely his. The crooked cross is seen everywhere.
Eventually, with the help of his splendid allies,
Europe will bow the neck to him and the entire
world will kneel before him. Constantly his people
hear the glad news of further triumphs on land, sea
and in the air . . . over burning deserts, over
snow-clad peaks, everywhere!

Even now he is standing, surrounded by his wise
counsellors, over a huge map. His finger points here,
points there. Stern faces relax into grim smiles.
'Tomorrow, the world!'

For myself – at any moment, surely, I will find
the opportunity to transfer myself from the woman
to the Leader. That done, I must rest. I will
go into Recharge. Why not? There is nothing
to report to the Cluster other than the victories
achieved by the Leader. They must know of these
already, of course. And, possibly, I shall be wise to
keep silence. The Cluster does not like its units to
choose their own paths. It was not my fault the
General was killed – and I cannot resist the hope of
rejoining the Leader, even without the Cluster's
approval.

So: I shall rest for a year or two. When I wake, I
shall once again glory in the victories and triumphs
that inevitably lie ahead for him, the Leader.

★　　★　　★

Everything is wrong, hopelessly wrong! I don't understand. It is Earth-year 1945, that is definite. I have been in Recharge for a long time and it is now 1945. And everything is wrong, wrong, wrong.

It is all a nightmare. I ask the Cluster to explain but it seems to share this evil dream. It tells me wrong things. They must be wrong, surely? How can the Leader *fail*?

Wrong, all wrong . . . It is like being in one of the storms that threatened to sweep us off our own planet – the storms that decided the Cluster to leave. Sudden storms. They whip and flurry the dark dust, fling bolts of raw energy, howl and bully and batter till even the mind of the Cluster cries 'No more! We surrender!'

That is what it is like inside the mind of the Leader. A hideous storm. Yes, I got back to him. I am in him again. In his mind.

But his mind is Chaos. Whipped to pulp by the storm.

How is that possible? What is happening? His body is sick, very sick. That I can understand; human bodies are too big, too complicated, too frail. But that mind of his, surely that cannot fail?

It is all a nightmare. Even the place I am in, even that is unreal. Look at it!

A raw, concrete bunker! An underground hiding place! A last resort! A place in which electric lamps flicker as the distant explosions come nearer, always nearer . . . and the ceilings shudder and let fall pale grey dust, grey as the human faces . . . and frightened men arrive with frightening messages . . . and terrified men sneak away, never to be seen again . . .

Where is the Leader's palace? Where are the parades? Where have they gone, those brazen trumpets, scarlet banners, glossy black jackboots?

And here is the woman again, the Leader's woman, big and pale and blonde and stupid. She dares to approach him! – to touch his shoulder with her painted nails! And he lets her! She says, 'A bite, just take a bite, to please me,' – and he obeys! He takes the food with trembling hands and puts it to his loose, dry mouth. He rolls his sunken eyes upwards to her face . . .

At least he does not attempt to smile. A smile, on that ravaged face!

She goes. The food falls uneaten from his shaking hand – or was it shaken by that latest, nearest explosion? The ceiling showers down dust. He touches the dust and examines it on his finger. Do his dead eyes see it? His cheek twitches. More explosions, ever nearer. Still he stares at the dust and still his cheek twitches, twitches, twitches.

No, none of this is real, it cannot be! This is not the Leader. Lies, all lies.

Wait. I will slide myself away from the source of

the lies. I am in one of his eyes and his eyes must be the liars. I will ascend to his brain, the truth will be there. I must have the truth.

I am sliding. Inwards. Upwards.

Nearly there. I can feel the vibrations of his mind, hear it 'talking'. 'This is a revolver,' it seems to be saying. 'I am holding a revolver. It is nearly time.'

That makes no sense. Slide closer in.

Now I am there, in the greatest mind of the greatest Leader of our Galaxy! Now for the vital truth!

And having learned it – many years from now, when the frail body of the Leader is enshrined in a mighty tomb and the flags wave over it and the sad bugles mourn – then will come my time of glory. I shall be in control. I will be that great mind and I shall bend it to my own will and purpose.

I mean, of course, the will and purpose of the Cluster.

What is his mighty brain telling me? What is it saying?

'The revolver,' he mutters. 'It is time . . .'

No, please, this is wrong!

'Eva, pity me!' he mutters.

Wrong, wrong!

He echoes my thoughts. 'Wrong, all wrong,' he mutters.

No, please! Don't! Take your finger from the trigger!

*   *   *

The body of Adolf Hitler, dictator, conqueror and mass-murderer, was found by advancing Allied troops soon after Hitler's suicide.

He administered poison by capsule to the wife he had recently married – Eva Braun – then shot himself.

As instructed by him, his body was carried up from the bunker to the Chancellory garden to be incinerated. So desperate were conditions in Berlin that not enough petrol could be found to fuel the fire. The body was incompletely burned.

ALIENS DON'T EAT
BACON SANDWICHES
by Helen Dunmore

My brother Dan has been making his own bacon
sandwiches since he was ten years old. It's not that
he likes cooking that much – it's just that no-one
else knows how to make the perfect bacon sandwich.
He'd get everything ready by the cooker first. Bacon,
bread, tomatoes, ketchup, sharp knife. The bacon had
to be fried fast, so it was crisp but not dried up. He'd
lay it on one slice of soft white bread, smear it with
ketchup, cover it with tomato slices, and then clap a
matching white slice on top. Then he'd bite into it
while the bacon was hot and the fat was soaking into
the bread. Dad used to say that Dan would go to
Mars and back if he thought there'd be a bacon

sandwich at the end of it. Don't forget this. The bacon sandwich is important.

Then there was the portable telephone. We should never have bought it, Mum said. I mean, I like talking to my friends on the phone, but Dan was something else. He was never off it. When he came in from school he'd pick up the phone right away and call someone he'd only been talking to half an hour before. And they'd talk and talk and talk. Sometimes Mum would come in and stand there tapping her watch or mouthing 'phone bill!' at him, but it never seemed to make much difference. Dan was a phone addict. I was cleaning my bike in the garden one day, and Mum and her friend Susie were talking about telephones and big bills and teenage kids. Susie said, 'It's all right as long as you realize that teenagers aren't people at all really. They're aliens from outer space. That's why they spend all their time on the phone. They have to keep in contact with other aliens who come from the same planet.'

I didn't take much notice of what Susie said at the time, but it came back to me later. Mum leaned back in her deckchair and laughed. She'd been out on a location all day, taking photographs: Mum's a photographer. She was working on a feature about corn circles. I expect you've seen pictures of them. Perfect circles in wheat, much too perfect to have been made by wind or rain. There were more of

them than ever that year, and nobody knew how
they came. At first the newspapers said it was a hoax.
Reporters and photographers used to sit up and keep
watch all night by cornfields, to catch the hoaxers.
But they never did. Somehow they'd get sleepy and
doze off and then when they jerked awake the circle
would be there, just as round as if it had been drawn
with a compass. Mum could have stayed the night
too. She was working with a journalist friend who'd
brought a tent along. Mum talked to Dan and me
about it, then she decided not to stay. It was just a
feeling she had that it wasn't a good idea. Dan and
I always listened to Mum when she got feelings about
things. Even I could remember how she'd said to
Dad, just before he went on that last trip, 'Do be
careful, love. I've got a feeling about it . . . I wish
you weren't going.'

Dad had worked for INTERSTEL airways, on the
crash investigation team. He was an instrument
specialist. This time he hadn't been investigating a
crash, but several pilots had reported interference
with their instruments over the Mojave Desert.
They'd managed to correct the problems manually
so far, but the airline was quietly panicking. Dad had
been working on a computer model, trying to find
some pattern in what was going on. I don't remember
much about that time, but Dan told me later that
Dad had been up most of the night the week before
he left. He was really worried. All he said to Dan and

Mum was that a pattern kept coming up, and he didn't like the look of it.

Mum's feeling was right. Dad's plane crashed not far from Coyote Lake. Something went wrong with the instruments, they said: there'd been massive distortions caused by what looked like a powerful electrical storm. At least, that's what it looked like on the computer trace. But no storm showed up for hundreds of miles on the weather charts.

I asked Mum if she thought the corn circles really were made by aliens, like people said. She frowned, then she said. 'I don't know, Tony. I don't believe that the circles are made by UFOs landing. That would be much too obvious. The feeling I have is that we're being teased. Or tricked. As if someone – or something – is trying to distract us from what they're really doing.'

'What do you mean?'

'It's hard to explain, but try to put yourself in their place. If there really are aliens trying to get a foothold on our planet, I think they'd do it in a way we'd hardly even notice. There'd be changes, but not huge ones. After all there are millions of us on this planet, and only a few of them. They'd come in very gradually over the years. They wouldn't want to risk being noticed – not too soon.'

'We'd be bound to notice, though, wouldn't we?'

'Not necessarily. Think of burglars. Some break in through the front door with crowbars, but others come in pairs pretending to be insurance salesmen. It's not till long after they've gone that you realize one of them's nipped upstairs and taken all your valuables. If there *were* aliens they wouldn't want to seem different. They'd want to seem like us. Part of normal life.'

So Mum thought the corn circles were there to keep us busy. To stop us noticing what else was going on. I shivered.

Dan was fifteen and a half, and I was almost eleven. You wouldn't think we'd be friends as well as brothers, but we always had been. Dan told me things he'd never tell Mum. He knew I'd never grass on him. And if something made him sad he could tell me that too. He had a music centre for his fifteenth birthday, much better than the one downstairs in the sitting-room. He'd lie on his bed and I'd lie on the floor and we'd listen to his music and he'd tell me about what was going on with his friends; not all of it, but some. Enough. Dan had a Saturday job, so he always had money. And he'd talk to me about Genevieve. He knew I liked her. He'd had girlfriends before, but Genevieve was different.

That was another clue I didn't pick up straight-away. It was about five o'clock and Dan and I were home from school, but Mum wasn't back yet. The phone rang and I answered it. It was Genevieve. She asked how I was, the way she always did. She even remembered that I'd had to take my budgie to the vet, and asked if he was OK now. Then she said, 'Is Dan there, Tony?'

'Yes, I'll just get him.'

I turned round. Dan was lounging in the doorway, watching me.

'It's Genevieve,' I said, holding out the phone, but Dan didn't take it. He just kept on looking at me. It's hard to describe what happened next. I hadn't really been thinking about what was going on, because I was just doing something I'd done loads of times before, taking a call for Dan and passing it on to him. And since it was Genevieve I knew he'd be pleased. But he wasn't pleased this time. He didn't react at all. I felt as if I was searching Dan's face for someone who wasn't there, like you'd search an empty house for a light in the windows.

'It's *Genevieve*!' I hissed, thinking perhaps he hadn't heard, and wishing I'd pressed the silence button in case Genevieve had. But Dan just shook his head, very slightly, as if he was making fun of me. Or Genevieve. And I was left holding the phone.

'I'm sorry, Genevieve,' I gabbled, 'He just went out, I think. I mean, I thought he was here, but he isn't.' It must have sounded like a lie, but Genevieve isn't a suspicious sort of person.

'Oh, that's OK, Tony,' she said. 'I'll try again later. See you,' and she put the phone down. Her voice was just the same as always. You know how some people's voices make you feel that good things are about to happen? Genevieve had that sort of voice.

Dan's voice was cold and irritated. I couldn't believe I was hearing him right. 'I wish she'd stop bothering me,' he said.

'What?'

'You heard. I said I wish she'd stop bothering me. That girl really bugs me. If she calls again, say you don't know when I'll be back. No. Never mind. I'll take the phone.'

He held his hand out for it. Darkness looked out of his eyes, and blankness. There was no Dan there at all. He took the phone and held it up as if he was going to dial straightaway. The silver antenna poked out at the side of his head. I felt a shiver go through me. The antenna. Dan's dead eyes. Something scratched at the back of my mind, wanting to be let in:

'*That's why they spend all their time on the phone, so they can keep in touch with all the other aliens . . .*'

I stared at Dan and he stared back at me. Mocking, as if he knew something I didn't. And in a way . . . almost frightening. And then I heard Mum's key go into the front door lock.

Dan stopped looking at me. By the time Mum called hello to us, he was already on his way up the stairs, calling back 'Homework' as he went. That was strange, too. Dan usually made Mum a cup of coffee when she got in from work. His bedroom door banged with the sort of bang that tells everyone else

151

to keep out. I waited to hear the music; Dan always turned on his music as soon as he got into his room. But nothing happened. It was absolutely silent, as if there was no Dan in there at all.

That was the first evening Dan didn't eat supper. He'd been into Burger King with Alex on his way back from school. Mum didn't bother about it: she was tired and upset because she and her journalist friend had had an argument with their editor. The editor didn't like the idea of aliens coming in secretly while we were all busy with the corn circles. He wasn't going to run the feature unless they changed it.

The next day Dan said he had to finish a piece of coursework and could he take a sandwich and a glass of milk up to his room. I don't remember all the excuses for not eating after that, at breakfast and tea and supper. They were never the same twice. Dan had always been clever, but now he was cunning too. He emptied his wastepaper basket every day now, so there was no chance of Mum finding the sandwiches he hadn't eaten. It was hard to know how much Mum had noticed. She never said anything, and she carried on giving Dan dinner money as usual.

It was three nights after the phone call from Genevieve that I couldn't sleep. My bedroom was next to Dan's, but I hadn't been into Dan's room for three days. Have you ever seen two magnets fighting one another with an invisible forcefield between them? There was one of those forcefields at Dan's bedroom door. You couldn't see it, you couldn't touch it, but it was there. Even Mum found excuses not to go in there. She was collecting the dirty washing one afternoon when Dan was late home, and she said, 'I ought to have a sock-search under Dan's bed,' but she didn't go in. She hesitated by his door, then she said, 'No. He's old enough to sort out his own dirty washing,' and she walked past into my room to change my duvet cover.

I kept turning over and over in bed. I was used to falling asleep to the sound of Dan's music, and I couldn't settle down in the silence. What was he doing? Was he sitting there? Reading? Working? I knew there wasn't anyone else in his room, though usually Dan had his friends round a lot, and often they stayed late. None of his friends had been round for the past three days. And I don't know what he'd said to Genevieve, but she hadn't called again. I tossed back the duvet and it flumped on to the floor. I found myself tiptoeing across the carpet, easing the door-handle down, pulling the door open very gently. The landing light was on. Everything was quiet and Mum's door was shut too. 12:37 on my watch. She'd be asleep. My heart thudded as I crept close to Dan's door. Yes, it was still there, the invisible hand pushing me away, saying I wasn't wanted there. But I wasn't going to take any notice this time. This was Dan, my brother. I took a breath, and touched his door-handle. Something fizzed on my fingers, like a tiny electric charge, like a rush of static electricity. I pulled my hand away and stepped back. Then I stopped myself.

'It's only Dan,' I told myself fiercely. 'It's only Dan.'

This time the prickle of electricity wasn't so bad, or perhaps it was because I was expecting it. Very gently I pushed the handle down. It didn't squeak or click. Then I pushed the door. As it opened a narrow strip of light fell from the landing into the darkness of Dan's room. It lit up Dan's bed, which was opposite the door. It lit up Dan, who was sitting up on the bed, fully dressed, reading. Reading in the dark. It lit up Dan's eyes as he turned to me, not at all surprised, as if he'd been expecting me. As if he'd seen me through the door.

'Hi,' he said, and turned a page.

There was only one switch for the main light, and it was by the door. It was off. I opened the door wider, so that more light came in, and walked across to Dan's bed. Casually, I touched his bedside light. It was cold. It hadn't been on at all. He'd really been reading in the dark – unless he'd been pretending? Unless he was trying to trick me and he'd been sitting there with the book, waiting for me to come in? But then how had he known I was going to come in?

There wasn't an answer. There was only Dan

sitting on his bed. He didn't look as if he liked me much.

'I can't sleep,' I said. 'I'm going down to make some hot chocolate. Do you want some?'

'No,' said Dan. A week ago he'd have come down with me so I wouldn't make too much noise and wake up Mum. He'd have whipped up the chocolate, the way he does. Suddenly I had an idea.

'I'm going to make a bacon sandwich,' I said, and waited for Dan to say what he always said: 'You make a bacon sandwich? Don't make me laugh. Let the man from the army do it.' And then he'd make it for me.

He didn't. But something went over his face. Just for a second, there was a flicker of the real Dan, and as soon as I saw it I knew for sure that whoever else had been there the past three days, it hadn't been Dan. Then his face went back to the not-Dan face. The alien face. I felt the back of my neck prickle. Maybe it was the electricity, tingling around the room. Out of the corner of my eye I caught a movement. It was the minute hand of Dan's electric wall-clock, racing crazily round and round in a perfect circle. The thing inside my brother looked straight at me, daring me to say what I'd seen. The prickle ran up my arms and down. I'd run into a storm, just the way Dad had done, only here it wasn't as strong. There was only one of them here. I shook my head to clear the buzzing of my thoughts. Dan needed me.

'I really fancy a bacon sandwich,' I said again. 'We've got all the stuff. White bread, tomatoes, ketchup – and Mum bought some back bacon yesterday.'

Something struggled in his eyes again, like the ghost of my brother. It wasn't winning. Dan wanted so much to come back, but he couldn't. There was something else there, something alien, and it was too strong for Dan. It meant to stay, and it meant to keep Dan out of his own body. But at least now I felt I knew what I was fighting. What we were fighting. Dan hadn't eaten anything for three days. I knew he hadn't. He must be hungry. Whatever was in him now didn't need food, not our earth food. But Dan did. And Dan would do anything for a bacon sandwich. Perhaps, if I could take him by surprise somehow, and get him to eat – could that break whatever power this thing had over him? I didn't know, but it was worth trying.

'See you downstairs if you change your mind,' I said.

Our neighbours have a baby which cries in the night, so Mum goes to bed with cottonwool in her ears. Even so, I moved quietly as I lit the gas, got out the heavy frying-pan, found bacon and tomatoes in the fridge, rummaged in the cupboard for ketchup. I just hoped the smell of frying bacon wouldn't wake her. I put the frying-pan on, melted a bit of fat, and lowered the bacon on the slice. It fizzled. After a minute the first tantalising wisp of the smell of frying bacon began to wreathe round the kitchen. Soon it would be through the door, then up the stairs, then under Dan's door. I turned up the heat carefully. I didn't want it to burn. The bacon spluttered, making a friendly sound in the kitchen. I laid the bread ready, and the sliced tomatoes, and the ketchup bottle. A drop of hot fat sparked on to the back of my hand and I sucked it away. Dan. Dan. Dan.

'Dan'd go to Mars and back if he thought he'd get a bacon sandwich at the end of it,' Dad used to say. That was before Dad went.

The kitchen door opened. Dan walked slowly, as if he was pushing through something heavy. His face was pale, and it wasn't smooth and hard any more, the way it had been the past three days. It looked crumpled, as if he was trying to remember something.

'Your sandwich is nearly ready,' I said. I took the bacon off the heat, slid the slices out of the pan and laid them across the bread. I layered on the tomato and squeezed out just the right amount of ketchup. Then I cut the sandwich in half. Dan watched me all the time. I lifted my half, and took a bite. I saw him lick his lips, but he was shivering, as if he felt cold. And things were moving behind his eyes, as if they were fighting for space there.

'Dan,' I said. 'Your sandwich is getting cold.'

His hands had dropped to his sides. They looked heavy. He didn't have the strength even to lift his hands, because all his strength was going into that fight inside him, between the Dan who was my brother and the stranger who wanted to make his home inside my brother's body. And that stranger was hanging on, tooth and claw. It wasn't going to let go easily. I knew now for sure that it was nothing human that was looking at me out of Dan's eyes. It had come from far away, and all it cared about was its resting-place. It was here for a purpose. It didn't care for Dan, or me or any of us. All it cared about was what it needed. Dan would never eat or sleep again if it had its way.

'Dan,' I said again. It felt as if his name was all I had. I came up close to him with his half of the sandwich still in my hand. He backed off a step or two, but then he didn't go any farther. I knew it was the real Dan who wanted to stay.

Suddenly I remembered something from far back, when I was sick with tonsilitis, not long after Dad died. It was when I was about six, I think. I had to take medicine four times a day, and I hated it. I used to press my lips tight shut and Mum couldn't make me swallow it. Then Dan took the spoon. He didn't seem worried, like Mum, and he didn't have any doubt that I'd open my mouth. He just put the spoon near my lips, without trying to push it into my mouth, and he said, 'Come on, babes. Do it for me.' And I did, every time, four times a day till I was better. The words had been like magic to me then,

when I was a little kid. Would they work now? Could they be the one thing that would bring Dan back and help him to fight off that powerful and lonely thing which had come to make its home in him?

I held the bacon sandwich up to Dan's mouth. His face was sweaty and he was breathing hard, as if he'd been running a long way.

'Come on, babes,' I whispered. 'Do it for me.'

I held my breath. I said it again, but silently. Then, like something in slow motion, Dan's mouth opened. I could see how hungry he was. How much he wanted to come home. I felt the electric prickle again, the one I'd felt when I first tried to open Dan's door. It was stronger now. It was trying to beat up a storm. It was fighting me, as well as Dan. But this time it wasn't going to win. Dan bit down. He bit into the white bread, the bacon which was still hot, the juicy tomato. I saw the marks of his teeth in the bread. He chewed, and he swallowed the bacon sandwich. Then I looked at him and it was like looking at a house where all the lights have come on at once after it's been empty for a long time. His hands weren't heavy any more. He grasped the sandwich, bit again, and in a minute he'd finished it.

'You going to make me another, Tony, or have I got to show you how the man from the army makes a bacon sandwich?' he asked, and he smiled.

I didn't even jump when Mum opened the kitchen

door. I knew it was her, not the thing which had been here and which was gone now, away through lonely space and places I couldn't begin to imagine, looking for somewhere else to make its home. Mum pulled the cotton wool out of her ears.

'You boys,' she said. 'I should have known. I was dreaming about bacon sandwiches.'

I don't know how Dan made it up with Genevieve, but the next day she was round at our house again. Dan's bedroom door was open, and his music was throbbing through the house. Mum didn't tell him to turn it down. She was in a wonderful mood because the editor had rung her back. He'd changed his mind and he was going to run the story about the corn circles in the way Mum and her friend wanted. For some reason he'd suddenly come to think it was worth printing the theory about aliens operating like bogus insurance salesmen, distracting us with corn circles and stealing our valuables when we weren't looking.

I asked Mum, 'Does the editor have kids?'

'Yes, he's got a teenage daughter. She's been a bit of a problem lately, apparently – he was telling me.' Mum glanced round, saw Dan was laughing with Genevieve, and whispered, 'His daughter's been acting a bit like Dan has these past few days, I think. But he says she's got over it, too.'

Genevieve stayed to supper, and you can guess

what we ate. While we were eating it, I thought of what had happened the night before, in our midnight kitchen.

'Aliens don't eat bacon sandwiches,' I thought, looking at my brother.

PEACEMAKER
by Malorie Blackman

'Michela Corbin, what did I just say?'

The class began to snigger. I looked up dismayed. There, right in front of my desk, stood Teacher Faber. I stared up at her, blinking with confusion. I hadn't even seen her coming! I tried to cover my literature screen with my hand but the teacher was too quick for me. She snatched up my screen and started to read the story I'd been writing. I groaned. I was in deep, *deep* trouble. Again!

'Michela Corbin, you are supposed to be writing an essay on section four-one-five of the Peace Treaty between the Alliance and the Inthral Sector. Not this . . . this . . . *this*!' Teacher Faber waved my lit. screen under my nose with disdain.

'I'm sorry. I'll erase it.' I grabbed for my screen. Teacher Faber snatched it back.

'Let us take a look at what has so captured your attention,' said the teacher, her tone really sarcastic. 'Are you ready for this, class?' she asked. '*I spun around, quick as a Pogett snake. Davin lunged at me with her laz-sword. Immediately I swung my weapon down to parry her thrust. The sound of laser beam on laser beam zinged almost musically. With a furious roar, Davin whipped her laz-sword upwards towards my head. I ducked and stepped back simultaneously. I didn't want to hurt her but one touch from the laz-sword was lethal – and I wasn't about to die. I . . .*' Teacher Faber stopped reading, but not before my face was on fire. Half the class were in fits of laughter. The other half were glaring at me, disapprovingly.

'This tish-tosh is not just nonsense, it's dangerous nonsense. I told you the last time that you'd had your final warning. Now you'll go on report. Again,' said Teacher Faber with satisfaction.

'Oh please, you can't. My mother will go nuts! I'll do the essay. I'll stay behind and work late. I'll . . .'

'Not another word,' interrupted the teacher. 'You're on report and that's final. And I shall make sure that your mother sees this . . . this story of yours.'

My blood ran icy cold. 'You can't do that . . .' I whispered.

'Watch me,' said Teacher Faber. 'I don't know

what's wrong with you, Michela. You persist with writing these kinds of stories . . .'

'They're adventure stories,' I protested. 'They're just fiction . . .'

'You humans are supposed to abhor violence of any kind – even in stories,' said Teacher Faber. 'And yet Michela, you insist on reading forbidden books like *Treasure Island* and *The Three Musketeers* and on writing this kind of fantastical, dangerous foolishness.'

It wasn't my fault I read forbidden books. If they weren't forbidden in the first place, then I wouldn't get into trouble for reading them! Mother owned an impressive collection of nineteenth and twentieth-century fiction books, most of them now classified as forbidden. She kept them locked up in dura-glass cases and it'd taken me ages to get at them without Mother knowing. She called them 'a good investment' – whatever that meant. I called them a good read. I didn't see the point in owning books if you didn't read them. The trouble was, Mother didn't see it like that. I'd been caught with Mother's books more than once and the last time, Mother threatened to burn them all if I was caught with just one of them again. So instead of reading them, I'd taken to writing my own – but that seemed to get me into even worse trouble!

'I won't read or write any more,' I pleaded. 'Please don't report me.'

Teacher Faber keyed in some commands on the

console that was situated on her stomach. Her fingers moved so quickly, they were a blur.

'It is done,' Teacher Faber moved away. 'A full report has been transmitted to Commander Newton and to your mother.'

I scowled at her. Rotten, Pogett-brained, Valunian weasel! I groaned. What was my mother going to say?

'Teacher Faber sent me yet another demerit report on you today.'

'Mother, I can explain . . .'

Mother flopped down into her favourite recliner and kicked off her shoes. 'Michela, I don't want to hear it,' she sighed. 'I've reasoned with you, pleaded with you, argued until I'm blue.'

'It was only a story, Mother,' I said quietly.

'A story! Why can't you write stories about proper subjects? What's wrong with peace and diplomacy and friendship? Why must you revel in violence?'

'I don't,' I said furiously. 'They're only stories, Mother . . .'

'They're a way of thinking. They're a way of *being*,' my mother replied. 'You persist in embarrassing me in front of my colleagues. Think of what your father would say if he was still alive.'

And with that one single argument, Mother forced me to shut up and not argue.

An uncomfortable silence filled the room.

'Michela, have you been recoding your Peace-maker?'

'Of course not!' I blustered.

After the *Treasure Island* incident, I'd been sent to Doctor Bevan to have my Peacemaker checked out. Everyone had a Peacemaker permanently attached to the inside of their left wrist on their eleventh birthday. There were no exceptions made. The Peacemaker was a small, grey disk which looked like one of those old-fashioned buttons people used to fasten their clothes. Doctor Bevan explained that it was a behavioural inhibitor – supposed to ensure that the non-aggression we'd all been taught for the last century was more than just a lesson. The Peacemaker was supposed to make sure that it was physically impossible for us humans to be aggressive. No more wars, no more fights, we couldn't hurt each other any more. Only it didn't stop there. Books and films that had once been considered classics had now been banned. And more and more things these days were taken as signs of belligerence, like talking, laughing and singing too loudly – and as I do all three, I'm constantly on report! Take last feast day, for example. We had Caen-Hal flowers from Rigel-4 for dessert. Caen-Hal flowers are most people's favourite food, a treat we only have once a year because they're so difficult and expensive to grow. Jeanette Peters tried to pinch mine and because I protested I was put on report and hauled up in front of Mother.

'How come it's all right for Jeanette to steal my food but it's not all right for me to stop her?' I asked angrily.

'Jeanette was wrong too,' said Mother. 'But you were more wrong! Your reaction could have led to violence. And as my daughter, Michela, you should know better.'

And that was the problem really. I was always letting Mother down – and we both knew it.

Mother shook her head sadly. 'Why do you do it? I read your story, Michela. Is that really what's in your head – in spite of everything I've tried to teach you?'

'It was just a story, Mother,' I whispered un-happily.

'And the part where you were fighting with the laz–sword?' Mother asked.

'I put that in because it's the only weapon I've seen a hologram of,' I said.

'You told me that you wanted to train in Je-kan-ia for the exercise, to teach you balance and co-ordination. It's obvious what's in your mind as you use the Kan-ia – you pretend it's a real weapon instead of the plastic stick it is. I forbid you to practise that so-called sport in the future,' said Mother.

'But it's the only thing I'm any good at,' I protested. Don't take that away from me. Not that as well, I thought desperately.

'That's enough. You're not to practise Je-kan-ia any more and that's final.'

From the look on Mother's face, I knew she really meant it.

'And you can go to Doctor Bevan right this minute and get your Peacemaker checked out. And if you *have* been tampering with it . . .'

'CON ONE! CON ONE! Captain Corbin to the bridge immediately. Captain Corbin to the bridge.'

Mother was interrupted in mid-sentence. She slipped her shoes back on to her feet and within seconds she was out the door. I stared after her. What was going on? What had happened to take us from Condition Four – our usual state – to Condition One, which was only used for extreme, imminent danger? Usually the Cons moved up sequentially – not a jump from Four to One.

I was used to Mother, as captain of the ship, being called away at a moment's notice. At first it'd seemed exciting to have such an important mother – captain of the *Kitabu*, one of the most prestigious ships in the Alliance fleet. Recently the excitement had faded away to leave something else, something less noble, in its place. I hardly ever saw her. And it seemed to me that Mother was always Captain Corbin first and being my mother came a long way down the list. I didn't want to feel the way I did and I tried to stop myself but I couldn't help it.

'Come on, Michela,' I muttered, trying to pull

myself together. What should I do now? I glanced down at my Peacemaker. Whatever the emergency was, it'd saved me from getting into *real* trouble.

'What's going on?' I wondered out loud.

There was only one way to find out. I left the room and headed up to the bridge. Maybe I could sneak in without Mother seeing me.

But the moment I stepped on to the bridge, I gasped, then froze. There, directly in front of the *Kitabu* was the biggest ship I'd ever seen. Only a small portion of it filled the entire viewscreen. It must have had some kind of sensor-jamming device to appear before us like this without any warning.

There was no way anyone would throw me off the bridge. All eyes were on the colossal ship before us.

'Ensign Natsua, activate the universal decoder. Open a channel,' Mother said. She was standing before the viewer on the bridge, her face solemn. 'This is Captain Corbin of the Alliance ship, *Kitabu*. We come in peace. Our mission is to negotiate trade and route lines through this sector. Do you understand?'

Each encounter with a new alien species called for Mother or Commander Newton, her second-in-command, to issue a similar blurb. The idea was that the alien ship would analyze the words spoken, so that any further communication to them could be translated. That's the way our universal decoder worked as well.

Everyone on the bridge looked tense. This was always the worst moment of dealing with alien species.

After only a few moments, the alien ship disappeared off one half of my viewer to be replaced by the face and upper body of one of the alien crew. And such a face, I'd never seen before. My breath caught in my throat and refused to budge. The alien's face held only one eye in what was presumably its forehead. Its nose dominated its face, moving in a series of ridges downwards and outwards. It had lips – different from humans but similar enough to be recognizable as such. But the thing that made me stare without blinking, the thing that turned my stomach over was the alien's skin. It was transparent. I could see grey liquid running through tiny canals in its body. I could see the tops of two organs, one on either side of its upper body contracting and expanding. The two organs had to be the alien's hearts. The whole thing looked strange, bizarre – and totally disgusting!

'This is Captain Corbin of the Alliance ship, *Kitabu*. We come in peace. Do you understand?' Mother repeated. She didn't bat an eyelid at the look of the thing before her.

'I am Fflqa-Tur, a Chamrah knight. And I understand perfectly,' the alien replied. 'You have entered our sector without permission and must pay the price.'

'The price?' Mother questioned sharply.

'Our ships are now at war,' said Fflqa-Tur.

'We were not aware that permission was required. My ship is the first Alliance ship to enter this sector. We in the Alliance are peaceful, non-confrontational. We meant no harm.'

'Harm or not, it is Chamrah law. We are now at war.'

'We will not fight you.'

'You have no choice,' said the alien.

'We are prepared to leave this sector and never return,' said Mother.

'You cannot retreat,' Fflqa-Tur said. 'Your path lies ahead.'

Silence.

'Comms down,' Mother instructed the ensign. That way she could hear what Fflqa-Tur had to say but not vice versa. 'Lieutenant Dopp, what's the maximum speed of Fflqa-Tur's vessel?'

'Vel Five, according to our sensors,' the navigation officer replied.

'Comms up,' Mother ordered to resume two-way communication. 'Fflqa-Tur, I must repeat, we in the Alliance are peace-loving. We are peace-makers not war-makers. We will not fight with you. Our ship can travel at more than twice the speed of your craft. I am prepared to use that speed to withdraw so that our meeting does not end in violence.'

'Run if you must,' said Fflqa-Tur. 'But I will spend

the rest of my days searching for you throughout the galaxy until I hunt you down. The challenge has been issued. It is not yours to reject.'

'But this makes no sense. Why won't you let us leave? Why must we fight?' Mother asked, an edge creeping into her voice.

'It is our way. And if you leave, not only will our two ships be at war, but my people on Chamrah will be at war with your so-called Alliance,' said Fflqa-Tur. There was a pause before he added, 'I am also bound to inform you of an alternative option, as you did not deliberately break our laws.'

'I'm listening,' Mother said eagerly.

'You may send over your champion to fight against the best knight on my ship,' said Fflqa-Tur.

Mother's shoulders slumped momentarily. 'We have many champions – but not of fighting. Never of fighting.'

'Then how do you propose that we proceed with our combat?' asked Fflqa-Tur.

'As far as I'm concerned, we don't proceed at all. No-one on this ship will fight you. It's against everything we believe in.' Mother began to finger the necklace that Father had given her years before. It was her only sign of nervousness. I could almost hear her thinking, her expression was so intent. 'I have an alternative of my own to suggest.'

'Proceed,' the alien barked.

'We surrender,' Mother said, seriously.

Commander Newton sat up straighter in his chair. The ensign took a deep breath. No-one else on the bridge moved. Fflqa-Tur's expression was as unreadable and as immovable as a Earth monolith. He beckoned to one of his own bridge crew, and they whispered together for a few moments.

Fflqa-Tur turned back to the viewer. 'We are unfamiliar with the word "surrender". Explain.'

'It means we concede defeat, we submit, we yield. We will give ourselves over to you,' Mother said. 'We will not fight.'

Fflqa-Tur smiled. 'Your Alliance is worthless. A Chamrah baby has more courage, more valour. You will stand and fight. Or you will stand and die. The choice is yours. You have fifty locshans to prepare.'

Fflqa-Tur's image disappeared from the viewer to be replaced by his ship.

'Locshans?' asked Mother.

'A moment, captain,' said Lieutenant Dopp. Silence reigned for several seconds as the lieutenant manually keyed into the universal decoder. 'Fifty locshans would appear to be the equivalent of ten Earth minutes.'

'Ensign, open another channel. I've got to try and reason with them,' said Mother after a pause.

'They're not responding, captain,' said the ensign.

'Keep trying.' Mother went back to her seat.

'What do we do, captain?' asked Commander Newton.

'If they don't answer . . . we prepare to die,' Mother said, still staring at the viewer. 'We will not endanger the Alliance. *We will not fight.*'

'We could leave this sector,' suggested the commander.

'No. We're not going to run,' said Mother. 'I'm not going to let this escalate into a full-blown war between the Alliance and the Chamrah nation. We must try to get through to them, but if not . . .' Mother didn't say any more, she didn't have to.

I stared at her. Would she really let us all die, without even a fight? Looking around the bridge, everyone wore the same expression as Mother on their faces. I had my answer.

I looked down at my Peacemaker. How I wished I hadn't tampered with it. The others on the bridge were obviously prepared to do as Mother had said and die rather than go against their beliefs. Me? I wanted to fight. And the feeling was so strong that it scared me. What could I do? I was only thirteen.

'Mother, can I . . . ?' I began.

Mother's head whipped around. 'Michela, get off the bridge. You're not supposed to be up here.' She didn't even let me finish.

I looked at her. She looked at me, worry and resignation on her face. And at that moment, I knew it was hopeless. We were going to die. I turned away. Unexpectedly Mother called me back and hugged me. I clung to her, but all too soon it ended.

'Go to our quarters,' Mother said gently. 'I'll join you later.'

After a pause, I left the bridge without another word – but it wasn't to go back to our quarters. It was too late to wonder what I would've done and how I would've felt if I hadn't tampered with my Peacemaker. The point was, I had. And if Fflqa-Tur of the Chamrah wanted a fighter, he would get one.

'Shuttle pod three, you are ordered to identify yourself.' Commander Newton's voice echoed all around the small shuttle pod.

I didn't answer. I couldn't answer – not yet. Not until I had finished rejigging the remote control codes and the forcefield cycle. Once that was done, I opened a channel to the alien ship.

'This is shuttle pod three. I wish to speak to Fflqa-Tur.' I kept repeating the message.

'Michela? What do you think you're doing?' Mother's face appeared on the shuttle pod viewer to my right. Her expression was incredulous, her voice furious. 'Michela, bring that shuttle pod back to this ship at once.'

'I can't, Mother. Please don't try to stop me,' I said.

'Ensign Natsua, lock on to that shuttle pod and bring it back,' Mother commanded.

'I can't, captain. The remote control codes have

176

been changed. We can no longer control that pod,' the ensign replied.

'Then use the tractor beam to bring her back,' Mother snapped.

'Sorry, captain,' the ensign replied after a few moments. 'The pod's forcefield frequency has been recalibrated to cycle at random every few pico-seconds. I can't get a lock.'

'Michela, bring that pod back now and I promise we'll say no more about it. Running away from this ship isn't the answer. Your pod can't outrun the Chamrah. Your place is on this ship – no matter what happens,' said Mother.

I stared at her. I couldn't believe it. Did she really think I was trying to run away, to escape the *Kitabu*'s inevitable fate? Is that what she really thought of me?

'Bye, Mother,' I said quietly. And I switched off the viewer. I carried on sending out my hailing message to Fflqa-Tur.

Without warning his image appeared on my viewer. I swallowed hard.

'Fflqa-Tur,' I coughed to clear my throat. 'Fflqa-Tur, I am Michela Corbin of the Alliance ship, Kitabu. I have come to accept your challenge.'

Fflqa-Tur's eye narrowed. 'You are a human?'

'Yes.'

'You are a knight?'

'Not as such.'

'You are a warrior.'

'Not quite. But it doesn't matter what I am. I'm accepting your challenge,' I said.

There was a deathly hush. Then came a moment when every part of me, every drop of blood in my body, froze, as if I was suddenly plunged into a bath of liquid nitrogen. The next thing I knew I was standing directly in front of Fflqa-Tur.

'W-what happened?' I whispered.

Fflqa-Tur spoke to me but I didn't understand. I shook my head. Someone behind him came up to me and injected something into my ear. It was uncomfortable for a moment but it didn't hurt.

'You have been brought aboard our ship via our conveyor beam.' Fflqa-Tur spoke and this time I could understand every word. 'I wanted to see you for myself.'

'Well, here I am. What happens now?' I asked.

I felt so strange, so *calm*. For the first time, the enormity of what I was doing struck me. I was actually doing this. And unlike in one of my stories, I wouldn't be coming back. I'd never see my mother or the *Kitabu* crew again, but they would be safe and free.

And, as consolation, I was in the middle of an *adventure*. This was real. Not a fantasy I'd written out on my lit. screen. Not a dream in my head. Real.

'You will fight against the champion knight of my ship,' said Fflqa-Tur.

'Are you the captain of this ship?' I asked.

'I am.'

'Then I will fight against no-one but you,' I said quietly.

Fflqa-Tur stared at me. Then he started to smile. I wondered if the look on his face meant that he was impressed, although for all I knew it could have been indigestion.

'Your challenge is accepted,' said Fflqa-Tur. 'Let us go to the arena.'

'One last thing.' I swallowed hard, afraid I was pushing my luck. 'I'd like our fight relayed back to the *Kitabu*. I want my . . . Captain Corbin and everyone else on the *Kitabu* to see our contest.'

'Agreed,' said Fflqa-Tur. 'You will now come with me. You will be clothed as a Chamrah knight and you must select your weapon.'

The arena was a small circular pit only about five metres in diameter and filled with what felt like Earth sand, only dark green in colour. Others like Fflqa-Tur sat around the arena. Funny, but they didn't look so disgusting any more. In fact they looked noble. I supposed that, given time – and the right frame of mind – you could get used to anything.

Shouts and cheers filled the air. In walked Fflqa-Tur. He was clothed as I was, in a neck-to-toe outfit that resembled an Earth-England medieval suit-of-armour, but the Chamrah version was almost transparent, very light and comfortable. In his hand

Fflqa-Tur had what looked like a pendulum on a stick. For my weapon, I'd chosen the closest thing to a laz-sword I could find. This one was more primitive – solid metal but with a laser-sharp edge. It wouldn't have made much difference what I'd chosen really. I had never faced a real opponent in my life. An instructor robot programmed for Je-kan-ia had been my teacher. But a robot's programming would be no match for a knight skilled in the use of Chamrah weapons.

Fflqa-Tur stepped into the arena. The crowd around us fell into an expectant silence. I looked around. Was Mother watching me now? I hoped she was. If she was, what was she thinking? I would have given anything to know. Here I stood, in the arena facing Fflqa-Tur – and even now it felt as if I was failing her. If only I'd left my Peacemaker alone – how much easier it would've been.

Fflqa-Tur raised his weapon and started moving towards me. Immediately, instinctively, I backed away, raising my sword between us. Fflqa-Tur and I circled warily around each other. My heart was about to explode from my chest. I could hear the blood roaring and rushing in my ears like a stormy sea. Fflqa-Tur lunged at me. Too terrified to even cry out, I leapt back. Staring at him, I took a deep breath, then another. Then I relaxed my grip on the sword. I'd been holding it so tightly that my fingers were turning numb. Slowly I stood up straight. I'd made

up my mind. I might lose, but Fflqa-Tur would know he'd been in a fight!

The battle between us lasted longer than I thought it would — a good forty-five seconds at least. That wasn't the only surprise.

I won.

Heart pounding, head throbbing, palms sweating, I won. My first two moves stopped Fflqa-Tur's attempts to lunge at me. With my third sword stroke, I knocked his weapon out of his hand. It sailed up into the air away from us. I thrust forward until the point of my sword was against Fflqa-Tur's body. He didn't say a word. No-one around us moved. The silence was deafening. I watched him, he watched me. Then I threw my sword down on the ground.

I waited anxiously, unsure what to do next.

There was a long pause. Then, without warning, Fflqa-Tur tilted his head back and laughed — or rather, he did what had to be the Chamrah equivalent. The others around the arena joined in, until the air was filled with their laughing.

'Is that it?' I asked, confused. 'What happens now?'

'Well done, little one. You have passed our test.'

'Test?'

'You accepted my challenge. You fought, but you did not kill,' said Fflqa-Tur.

'Test?' Then I realized. 'You let me win! But . . . but I could have killed you.' I stared at him.

Fflqa-Tur beckoned to one of his crew. The crew

member left his seat and came into the arena. He picked up the weapon I had just thrown on the ground. Before I could stop him, before I could even cry out, he lunged at Fflqa-Tur. I watched, wide-eyed with horror as the sword blade passed right through Fflqa-Tur's body. The captain didn't even flinch. In fact he laughed again at the look on my face.

Then I saw what had happened. All the canals filled with grey liquid and one of Fflqa-Tur's hearts had moved out of the way of the sword. They had all shifted to be either above or below the blade.

'Every part of me has a life of its own,' explained Fflqa-Tur. 'And they could see the sword coming.'

'But I don't understand. Why this test?' I said slowly, trying to take it in.

'We Chamrah have to choose our friends carefully. We are a peaceful race. We do not want aggressors as friends. Nor do we want aggressors using our trade routes. But we do not want cowards as our friends either. You showed that you were prepared to fight for what you believed in, no matter what the outcome – but you didn't kill me. You could have done but you didn't,' said Fflqa-Tur.

'Because killing is wrong,' I said.

'Then why did you accept the challenge?' Fflqa-Tur asked.

'Because . . . because it seemed to me that sometimes . . . sometimes you have to take a stand, even if you know you're going to lose.' I frowned. 'And I couldn't let you destroy our ship and kill all those people, not when I thought I could do something about it. How could I sit back and not do something about it?'

'You are indeed very brave,' said Fflqa-Tur. 'And bravery is everything.'

Bravery . . . Would Mother see it that way? But then a strange thought occurred to me. By refusing to kill, but not running away, didn't Mother do exactly what I was doing now? In her own way Mother was just as brave as Fflqa-Tur. Only I'd never realized it before.

'Can they still see me on the *Kitabu*?' I asked.

'Yes.'

I turned to the viewer. 'Mother, I need to see Doctor Bevan. I did recode my Peacemaker, but don't worry. I won't tamper with it any more.'

'Peacemaker?' said the captain.

So I explained.

Fflqa-Tur said, 'But you have proven that you do not need to wear such a device. You were prepared to fight and die for your ship and your comrades, but you weren't prepared to kill needlessly. You showed compassion. That was all we needed to see.'

I looked down at my Peacemaker . . . and wondered.

'I will escort you to my bridge. You will be sent back to your ship from there,' said Fflqa-Tur.

As we walked back, I turned to the captain and said, 'Fflqa-Tur, may I keep my weapon and armour? As a souvenir?'

Fflqa-Tur nodded. 'Will you be punished when you return to your ship?' he asked.

'I should think so,' I sighed. Thoughts of the essays I'd have to write and the endless lectures I'd have to listen to filled my head.

'Is there no-one on your ship who will be proud of you?' asked Fflqa-Tur.

'I . . . I don't know.' I shrugged.

Somehow . . . somehow I thought that Mother would understand. But even if she didn't, it wouldn't matter.

'I'm proud of myself,' I said at last. 'And that's enough.'

A SELECTED LIST OF TITLES
AVAILABLE FROM CORGI BOOKS